PROLOGUE

The girl angrily slammed the magazine shut and flung it on her bed. Suddenly she felt eleven years old again, and it all came flooding back to her. Not that she'd ever really forgotten. She'd wanted to ride so badly, to see those beautiful ponies every day. She'd been desperate to learn, and she would have tried her best, if they'd just given her a chance. And all it had taken was a phone call lasting barely thirty seconds to crush her dream. There hadn't been another opportunity after that. She remembered sitting on the steps at home, still in her riding boots, crying like she'd never stop. She couldn't stop thinking about the girl, the way she'd looked at her like she was nothing and couldn't even be bothered to talk to her. She got a rush of anger when she thought about the girl's dismissive expression. She hated her.

Picking up the magazine again, she studied the photo and felt the same rage start to build up. The other girl's popularity kept growing. But one day soon, she'd pay...

Chapter 1

There she was again.

Alice Smalley just had time to make out the bright pink of a T-shirt before the girl flew back round the corner, peering out from behind the old wall next to the shop. Her big dark eyes gazed at Secret as Alice checked the traffic ahead and pushed Secret into a trot to make it round the parked cars before the oncoming tractor met them.

When she glanced back, the girl had gone. Alice had seen her nearly every time she'd ridden out for the past few weeks, but by the time she was in a safe position to stop the girl was out of sight.

Reaching the drive back to Park Farm, where she lived with her mum and dad, Alice kicked her feet out of the stirrups and gave Secret a loose rein as he headed happily back up to the yard where the cool of his stable awaited, away from the relentless heat that gripped the country. As they headed into July, all the weather reports predicted the hottest summer on record, which was fine, Alice thought, if you didn't have yard jobs to do and a pony to keep fit for a busy summer of showjumping! She'd taken to setting her alarm early and getting out on Secret long before breakfast, which is why she'd been surprised to see the girl also up and about.

A beep from her pocket broke through her thoughts and, pulling her phone out, she smiled

as she opened a picture message from her friend Finn, who was spending the summer in Spain as part of the Rebel Riders stunt team, training with them at their base in Andalusia. Finn and Alice, who'd met when Secret had bolted out across a showground, had been through a lot and he was still one of her closest friends. But now he wasn't around and so even with her busy training schedule it could get a little lonely in the yard. Alice's mum, Josephine, one of the country's top showing producers, had also lost Finn as a rider, but Alice knew his heart belonged with the display riding and not in the show ring. Just as hers belonged in the showjumping arena.

"Nice ride?" Alice's mum greeted her with a smile as she led her own mare, Ella, back up to the yard after a night out in the fields. Ella was a rescue pony, brought back from Spain by Finn and his dad, Angus, who was Alice's showjumping

5

coach at Hilltops pony club.

"Great." Swinging lightly off Secret, Alice chuckled as he rubbed his head against her. Despite the high temperatures, Secret, who was in peak condition, had barely broken a sweat.

"Alice!" her mum chided gently. "You know you shouldn't let him do that. Bad manners!"

"I know," Alice grinned. "But it *is* Secret." Then she remembered what she had been meaning to ask her mum. "Did anyone move to the village recently?"

"I wouldn't know." Josephine shrugged. "Why do you ask?"

"Oh," Alice said. "No reason really."

They'd reached the stables now and Alice's mum had put Ella into her stable, slipping off her head collar as she gave her neck a stroke. Alice thought back to the girl and wondered who she was. She'd try to stop and say hello next time she spotted her.

★

"Hey, Alice!"

Amy, one of Alice's friends at the Hilltops pony club, bounded over. Alice was at the equestrian centre for her weekly team training with Angus. When she wasn't riding she often hung out at the café on site with other members. Hilltops had almost become a second home. The café had cosy sofas covered with Newmarket blankets, and having a hot chocolate there with friends after lessons had become one of the highlights! Hilltops was close enough to home that Alice could ride over during the summer months, and she had enough time before her lesson to give Secret a break and get herself a cold drink.

Amy fell in step with Alice as she headed back over to Secret in the shade.

Amy grinned and pulled out her phone. "I've had over a hundred messages today asking how

Secret is. Everyone loved that picture of him opening the gate!" She passed the phone over. "Here, have a read."

Alice took the phone, scrolling through the comments. It *was* a particularly cute photo of Secret, catching him at his cheekiest, his eyes full of mischief as he fiddled with the gate latch.

Just then a new comment flashed up at the top of the screen. Alice could only read the first few words.

Bet she thinks...

Alice frowned, passing the phone back. She didn't want to accidentally see any of Amy's messages; perhaps it was a school friend.

"Think you have a message," she said. "It just came up."

Amy took the phone, and then paused, peering at the screen with a frown.

"What's up?" Alice looked over at her friend

curiously as Amy squinted at her phone and then tapped it a few times, before giving Alice a bright smile.

"Oh," she said in a cheerful voice, "nothing. Just get some weird spammy messages sometimes. Here, look, you can read the rest!"

Alice skimmed through some more of the comments.

You're my favourite, Secret!

Aw, adorable.

Love that pony!

They were from all over the county, girls and boys who followed Secret's every move via his very own account. Using Alice's photos and Amy's witty captions, Amy had unofficially appointed herself as president of Secret's fan club, something Alice was both grateful for and baffled by! When Amy had first suggested they set up an account just for Secret, Alice had been sceptical, but her friend had been so insistent that she'd given in. Alice barely had enough time to reply to Finn half the time, let alone respond to hundreds of messages from strangers. Ever since his big win at Olympia Horse Show and his heroic antics during his stay in London, Secret had become quite the celebrity. His win had been enough to catapult him into the spotlight, but he'd also gained thousands of fans for his bravery during a kidnapping, where he had not only saved two other ponies, but also helped to uncover a fraudulent pony-selling ring. He'd taken part in a parade with the mounted police at the big Christmas show, and in the months since Alice felt as though life had been a whirlwind.

"That's nice." She smiled and handed the phone back to Amy, and started to tack Secret up. "Sorry for all the work."

"Are you joking?" Amy grinned, her eyes sparkling. "I LOVE it. And look, another interview

request from *Pony* mag, and someone asking if Secret can open the new saddlery in Matterley. You're in demand!"

Alice shook her head, totally bemused by it all. Although she had to admit it was kind of cool too. Secret's cheerful and cheeky personality combined with his winning ways had gone down a storm. Alice still couldn't believe how far they'd come.

Secret had always been special. He had helped Alice find her way again after her beloved first pony died, when she hadn't wanted to see another horse ever again. First she'd tried showing Secret, as her mum had wanted her to, and it had been a total disaster. So they'd turned their hand to showjumping, which had always been Alice's dream, and after a rocky start Secret was now tipped to be one of the country's leading pony showjumpers. What a feat for the pony who'd famously once refused to trot in a ring, and who'd thrown Alice at her very first ridden event with him! Secret adored jumping – he was fast and nimble and his scope knew no bounds. Now that Alice had learned to cope with his strength and enthusiasm, they were unstoppable. Secret gave her the confidence she lacked in day-to-day life, and Alice knew she owed him everything.

"Anyway, you'd better get on, Angus is here." Amy gave her friend a quick hug. "Word going round is there's something exciting he wants to talk to us all about. Something about a big show. I'd better get tacked up!"

Alice was up and in the saddle in an instant, hugging Secret before gathering up her reins and heading towards the indoor school, eager to hear the news.

Chapter 2

"Ok, everyone, listen up!"

Angus leaned against one of the jump wings as he addressed the three pony clubbers gathered before him, Alice, Amy and Jordan, one of the few boys in the branch. Hilltops was a small club, and with everyone interested in different things – cross country, dressage, the Prince Philip Cup – it had been hard at times to get enough people interested in pure showjumping. For a while it had become really popular, but exams and school and other hobbies had started to crop up and numbers had decreased. But they'd had some good results as a pony club so far, and despite their small size the branch was starting to make a name for itself.

"I thought we all needed something to focus on this summer," Angus continued as everyone glanced at each other. "What do you say to putting forward a team for the pony club competition at Hickstead?"

Alice sat up a little straighter in her saddle, feeling a jolt of excitement at the mention of one of the most famous showjumping arenas in the world. "Hickstead?" she repeated, grinning.

Alice knew that on the final day of Hickstead the pony club held a competition for branches, with the qualifying teams on the day getting the chance to jump in the main arena.

Angus nodded with a smile. "That's right. The very one! I think Hilltops as a branch should take it up a level, don't you? We might be small, but we're more than capable!"

Alice grinned. "For sure!"

Jordan, next to her, whooped in delight. "So cool!" he said enthusiastically. "I did have football trials that week, but I'd rather jump."

"Great! I've got to send in all the paperwork this week before the closing date," Angus continued. "Alice, are you going to be at Hickstead for the showing classes?"

Alice nodded. "With Porridge. We're hoping he'll be in the junior ridden class. But that's only if Mum can find someone to ride him."

Porridge was her mum's Shetland pony, who'd qualified in the junior class with the daughter of one of Josephine's clients. But the little girl had also qualified her own pony and she couldn't ride both. Alice's mum was really hoping to find a young rider for the class. Alice loved Porridge, and would have ridden him herself had she not been too old for the class ... and far too tall for Porridge!

"But who else will be on the team?" Amy asked. She was next to Alice on her gorgeous grey pony Whisper. "Don't we need four?"

Angus smiled. "That's another thing I was going to talk to you about. We've actually got a new member; she's just transferred over from Pembroke North. You may have jumped against her a few times. Chloe Williams?"

Alice frowned. The name was vaguely familiar but Alice tended to keep herself to herself at shows, either waiting in the lorry with her mum or concentrating on Secret. Quite often the effort of keeping the little red gelding focused and controllable meant she missed the comings

and goings of the warm-up ring and walking around on a loose rein chatting with the others in her classes. She'd never been to a social afterwards either, as Josephine liked to get straight home afterwards to sort out the ponies on the yard.

"Sounds good," Alice said. "Has she tried out?"

"Not exactly," Angus replied, "but she's got good results. I met her mum last week and we agreed she could transfer over and join the team."

Amy grinned. "Bring it on!"

Alice smiled too, caught up in her friend's enthusiasm. She couldn't picture Chloe Williams but she sounded like she had good form. And Hickstead was going to be amazing!

Angus soon had the riders trotting and cantering over a grid as he put the pony club members through their paces. Secret surged forward; his small stature never held him back even as Angus raised the last jump higher and higher. Secret whisked over it, his tail streaming behind him, his small pale feet tucked right up as he gave the jump plenty of space.

Alice could probably count on one hand the times Secret had knocked a pole from the wings; he was as careful as he was powerful, and so far she hadn't found the limit to his scope. The Festival of the Horse, Olympia and now Hickstead on the horizon – it felt like nothing could stop him. And it would be even better jumping as a team with her friends! Alice thought back to the day her mum had let her join pony club. It had been the best thing for Alice and Secret, and now they were all set to represent the branch at one of the biggest shows in the country!

★

Alice was still thinking about the Hilltops showjumping team as she passed the whitewashed row of cottages on the corner of the road that

led back up to her house after her lesson. Secret seemed to enjoy admiring his reflection in the windows as he passed and Alice chuckled, kicking her feet from her stirrups and stretching her ankles. In a world of her own, she was totally unprepared as Secret spooked dramatically, his head shooting up as he snorted like a dragon. Alice, not concentrating, tumbled neatly off him, landing on her hip in a patch of bleached grass, still clutching the reins. She jumped up, relieved she wasn't hurt. *That will teach me*, she thought grimly.

"What happened there, boy?" Alice asked Secret, but just then she caught a glimpse of a girl with a mass of curly dark hair racing round the side of the cottages. She didn't look as old as Alice, perhaps a couple of years younger. Alice heard a shouted apology as she disappeared from sight.

"Sorry, I'm so sorry!"

Alice frowned, realising it was the same girl she'd seen before. She brushed her jods off and stretched her legs. She wasn't hurt at all, and Secret was nudging her as if asking her what on earth she was doing out of the saddle.

"It's all right!" Alice called. "I'm fine – I wasn't concentrating!" She led Secret round the side of the cottages, but the girl had disappeared. Alice wanted to let her know all was OK, but with Secret growing impatient to get back home to his friends Alice had no choice but to swing herself back into the saddle and head off. Glancing behind her as she rounded the corner, she glimpsed a small anxious face in one of the upstairs windows, but it happened so quickly she wasn't sure if it was just her imagination.

★

The rest of the afternoon was spent on the yard, with more ponies to ride, fields to be cleared and

hay nets to be made up, so Alice had no time to dwell on either the mystery girl or Angus's news about Hickstead and a new team member.

The sun was still high in the sky as she finished making up the last of the feeds. She decided she would come back later to turn out the ponies for the night. Clipping Secret's special lock to his stable door so that he couldn't undo it and cause carnage, she headed towards the house for dinner, hungry after a day's hard work. Her mum was out judging and her dad was still at work, but Fergus, the head groom, was about.

Suddenly Poppy, the family's elderly dog, gave a bark, scrambling unsteadily to her feet. Alice frowned at the unfamiliar car heading up the drive, coming to a stop outside the yard gates. Alice usually got to know the cars that belonged to her mum's clients, who came to visit their ponies at training. Wiping her dusty hands on her jodhpurs, she approached the car as a lady with a slightly worried expression and black curly hair came forward.

"Hi!" Alice said, wondering how she could help. "My mum and dad aren't in right now…"

The lady smiled. "Actually, it's you I'm after," she explained. "Do you ride a reddish-coloured pony?"

"Yes?" Alice replied hesitantly. Secret had once got out and was found munching on prize-winning flowers in someone's carefully tended garden, so she was always wary when he was mentioned. But she knew he was safely in his stable right now, and he hadn't escaped the yard for ages!

The lady looked relieved. "Oh! I'm so glad you're OK!"

Alice must have looked confused, because the lady smiled again. "You fell from your pony earlier," she said. "My daughter Mia was waiting

to see you and rushed out, but she must have scared him."

Ah, Alice thought. The younger girl she'd seen. It was making sense now.

"Oh, I'm fine! It was my fault really. He spooks easily and I wasn't concentrating, so please tell your daughter not to worry."

"Thank you," she said. "She's been so upset, you see…" Her smile faded for a moment and then she seemed to shake herself. "Anyway. Sorry for disturbing you!" She started to head back to her car, but Alice frowned.

"Wait!"

The lady turned back to her.

"Does your daughter like ponies?" Alice asked.

The lady nodded and smiled. "Mad about them," she said. "I don't know where it came from, certainly not from me or her dad, but ever since she could talk it's all she's gone on about.

Where we used to live, in the city, she rode every week. She loved it – it was the thing she looked forward to most – but since we moved…" She paused. "I thought we might see more horses, but it's hard when you don't know anyone. We asked another lady who rode past once but she sort of dismissed us. Then my daughter saw you. She loves to just watch you ride past. She said your pony is famous!"

Alice felt humble. She knew how lucky she was to have been born into a horsey family. She also knew what it was like to be completely and utterly pony mad, and could only imagine what it must be like not to be able to spend time with ponies. Suddenly she had an idea.

"Tell your daughter to come up!" she blurted out. "She can come and see the ponies, if she likes. I mean, only if she wants to…" Her voice trailed off, and she worried she might sound

patronising somehow.

But the lady's face broke into a wide smile. "That would make her day," she replied happily. "I'll tell her. Thank you. Thank you so much!"

Chapter 3

Alice told her mum and dad about her conversation with the lady later that evening.

"Good idea, Alice," her dad nodded. "There's enough ponies up here to come and see!"

"That was nice of you," Josephine said, smiling, but she seemed distracted as she flicked through the pages of her diary.

"What's up?" Alice was sitting cross-legged in

the chair in her mum's office, an old wool rug that had once belonged to Blue, her mum's childhood pony, draped over the back. Rosettes crowded together along the tops of the walls like colourful bunting. They were mostly reds or the red, white and blue of a championship. Josephine's yard had been very successful over the years.

"Oh." Her mum pushed her glasses up into her sandy blonde hair. "It's just this business with Porridge. It would be such a shame for him to miss Hickstead after doing so well. I thought it would be easy to find a rider for him!"

Alice knew the black Shetland held a big place in her mum's heart. Most of the ponies that came and went from the yard were owned by other people, with only Ella the Spanish pony, Secret and Porridge owned by Alice and her mum. With Lachlan, the wise old Highland, now gone after an awful accident, the remaining three ponies were very special. Porridge had seen Alice through from lead-rein classes to first ridden and Alice looked back on those days with fond nostalgia, even though she'd never been that into showing. But she could see this meant a lot to her mum.

"I'll try again to think of someone," she said. "Maybe someone in pony club has a little brother or sister. I'll ask around next time I'm there."

"Thanks, Al," her mum smiled, before changing the subject. "So, how did it go at training today? Angus has been in touch about Hickstead, and I think it's wonderful. You've always wanted to jump there!"

"I know!" Alice nodded enthusiastically.

It felt good knowing her mum was totally on side with Alice's jumping career. Initially her mum had been disappointed that Alice hadn't wanted to show Secret, but now she completely supported the two of them. With each new adventure she and

Secret were achieving far more than she'd ever dreamed of. She couldn't wait to see the emerald-green turf of Hickstead between his red ears!

★

Later that week Alice rode over the downs for another team training session. During the term Angus held the sessions as late as possible after school to allow the heat to subside, but it was still stiflingly warm as Alice made her way into the yard at Hilltops. There was a shiny new trailer parked up, and Alice assumed it must be Chloe Williams's, the latest addition to the pony club and the Hickstead team! Tied up outside and munching on a hay net was a lovely dapple-grey pony, about the same height as Secret but chunkier in build. He was tacked up and ready to go, a head collar over his bridle. Looking at him Alice couldn't help but imagine the Hilltops team cantering around during the lap of honour in the main arena at Hickstead. Then she shook her head. She was getting carried away! But Chloe's pony was gorgeous, and if he was as talented as he was handsome, her mum was right, this could be Hilltops' year.

There wasn't time to go and get a cold drink before the lesson, so Alice took a swig from the water bottle in her rucksack before heading over to the big jumping arena. Secret's step quickened, as if he knew what lay ahead. Despite having just been ridden for twenty minutes over the downs, he was raring to go.

Just then, a girl emerged from the trailer where the dapple grey was, giving the pony a hug and smoothing her long dark ponytail. It had to be Chloe. Alice decided to ride over to say hi and show her where the school was.

As she approached, the girl slipped the pony's head collar off, tightening her girth and then swung

herself into the saddle. Alice smiled, wondering if Chloe was feeling nervous. Alice never enjoyed being the new girl, and she still shuddered when she thought about her first day at senior school and her first lesson at Hilltops when she hadn't been able to control Secret.

"Hey!" she said in what she hoped was a bright and welcoming voice. "You must be Chloe?"

The girl looked up from adjusting her stirrups and stared straight at her. She was as tall as Alice but as dark-haired as Alice was fair, with a smattering of freckles across her pale skin. Her eyes were startlingly blue. She didn't smile back.

"Yes, I'm Chloe," she answered, and Alice frowned. She thought she recognised her, those deep blue eyes, that serious, watchful expression. "And I know you. Alice with the famous Secret."

There was something about her tone that Alice couldn't put her finger on.

"That's us." Alice tried to make a joke. "Secret's so famous he thinks he should be signing autographs somewhere, not at silly pony club…" And then she instantly regretted her words because Chloe raised an eyebrow.

"That was a joke." Alice felt a little flustered. "Sorry. He doesn't think pony club is silly."

"Yeah, I guessed that it was." Chloe looked at Alice as if she had just said the most obvious thing in the world.

She doesn't seem very friendly, Alice thought. Maybe she was really nervous. It was quite a big thing transferring from one branch to another.

There was a pause.

"Well, do you want to head to the lesson with me?" Alice asked, feeling slightly uncomfortable. "I'll show you where to go."

Chloe gathered up her reins and followed Alice towards the school, riding in silence behind her.

Alice kicked herself. She couldn't help but feel they'd got off to a bad start.

★

Angus had been right: Chloe and her pony, Mac, were good contenders for the team. Mac was an obvious schoolmaster and despite it being his first time in with the Hilltops ponies, he remained steady and calm, flying over everything in sight. *Unlike Secret's first time*, Alice thought wryly. As Chloe and Mac approached the double Angus had prepared to sharpen their stride technique, Alice watched a little more closely. If she had to be really critical, she'd say that Mac was the more experienced of the pair, forgiving Chloe for her slightly clumsy riding.

Amy, watching next to Alice, turned to her friend as Angus chatted to Jordan on the other side of the arena.

"She only started riding recently," Amy said in

a low voice. "Quite good, don't you think? Her mum was telling mine all about it."

Alice nodded, feeling guilty. If Chloe really had only been riding for a short while, she'd done brilliantly to get to where she was. And with Angus's expert tuition Chloe would improve in no time.

"That *is* good," she agreed. "I wonder why she started so late?"

Amy shrugged. "Not everyone is born in the saddle like you, Al!" she teased, but she was smiling. Alice thought again how lucky she was. She was totally pony mad, but because her mum was horsey it had been easy for her to immerse herself in it all.

"I know they moved house and she got into riding then," Amy continued. "I expect we'll find out more when we get to know her. She seems really nice, though, doesn't she?"

Alice swallowed, remembering her silly joke. Chloe must have thought she was so arrogant!

"I only met her before the lesson," she said carefully, "but yes."

And as she watched Chloe and Mac jump the double again, Mac guiding his rider through each and every stride, she frowned, once again thinking about those serious, startlingly blue eyes. She recognised Chloe from somewhere, but where?

★

Alice had been so busy with team training as well as revision for her end-of-year exams that she had almost forgotten about her conversation with the young girl's mum the previous week. And so she jumped as a friendly voice called hello as she washed out feed buckets one hot afternoon.

As she crossed the yard to let the lady and her daughter in, she wished she didn't look quite so hot and sweaty, a smudge of Mollichaff on her grubby T-shirt from where Secret had nudged her adoringly straight after his breakfast.

The woman smiled. "Hello! I don't think I ever told you my name when I came the other day. I'm Dominique, and this is Mia."

Dominique had her arm round Mia, and Alice noticed she gave her a gentle nudge forward. Mia was obviously shy, Alice thought sympathetically. She knew the feeling.

"Hey." Alice gave a little wave.

Mia smiled, dropping her gaze. "Hey," she said, her voice quiet.

Alice wasn't sure what to do next. "Um," she said slightly awkwardly, "do you want to come and meet the ponies?"

Mia nodded, her smile widening.

Leading the way, Alice took Mia and her mum over to Ella's stable, where the sweet grey mare was dozing in the shade. Once terrified of people,

Ella gently sniffed Mia's hands and neatly braided hair, making the young girl giggle as Ella's soft bristly whiskers tickled her ears.

"Ella was a rescue pony," Alice explained. "She finds it hard to trust people but she obviously likes you."

Mia looked delighted and Alice felt herself warming to her.

"Then this is Archie, one of my mum's clients' ponies, and that's Hendricks." She pointed out a lovely Welsh section C her mum had in for schooling, before moving down the line of stables, introducing each pony along the way.

"Then this –" she smiled as Secret popped his head over the door, eager to see who the new visitors were – "is my pony. His name is—"

"Secret!" Mia gave a little gasp before Alice could finish. "It's Secret, Mum, look!"

Dominique smiled. "Mia's got his poster up on

her wall," she explained. "When she saw you ride past, she couldn't believe it! Could you, Mia?"

Mia shook her head. Her shyness seemed to be disappearing now. She obviously adored horses and Secret was delighted with the attention he was getting from her.

"I'm really sorry about spooking him the other day," Mia said, biting her lip. "I didn't mean to."

Alice smiled. "Honestly, it's fine," she said. "I've had way worse falls off him in the past."

"Like the one at the country fair?" Mia replied enthusiastically. "I read you fell off and landed in horse poo, and Secret galloped away!"

Alice had recently been interviewed by a popular horse magazine and had recounted her first show with Secret. "Exactly!" she laughed. "See, way worse." She decided she liked Mia.

Then Mia's face lit up as a shaggy head popped over his custom-made door. Shetland pony

Porridge, his thick black forelock falling over his eyes, gave a little whinny as if reminding Alice not to leave him out.

"Oh!" Mia drew in her breath, her eyes sparkling. "Who's that?"

Alice smiled. "He's cute, isn't he? That's Porridge. But don't be fooled – he's no angel! Not quite as cheeky as Secret but he's feisty for his size!"

"Sounds like someone I know." Dominique gave her daughter an affectionate nudge.

Alice smiled as she saw Mia skipping towards Porridge's stable where the little black Shetland greeted her enthusiastically. Mia threw her arms round Porridge's chunky neck, burying her face into the silken black mane. "I love him!"

Alice joined her, giving Porridge a stroke. "He's sweet, isn't he?" Then she had an idea. Porridge loved nothing more than being ridden, even if it was just for ten minutes around the farm, and Mia was petite, so would be absolutely fine on the stocky Shetland.

"Would you like to ride him?" she asked, looking at Dominique and wondering if it was OK to ask. But Dominique just grinned and Mia jumped up and down with excitement.

"You bet!" she cried.

Chapter 4

It didn't take long to get Porridge tacked up and for Alice to find her old riding hat at the back of the tack room. She'd sent a quick text to her mum to let her know what she was doing and had received a *No problem, have fun!* message back. It was quite a change, Alice thought, shortening the stirrups on the little felt saddle. Her mum had always been extremely fussy about who was allowed on the yard. When Finn had come along it had taken a while for her mum to fully trust him with their ponies, despite his years of riding experience. But she was far more relaxed now, and Alice knew she completely trusted her judgement. She would clip a lead rein to Porridge's bridle and just walk him steadily around the fields.

Alice didn't think she'd ever seen a happier face than when Mia hopped up into the saddle, gathering up her reins and giving Porridge a scratch on the withers. She also noticed how nicely Mia sat, her back straight, her hands soft. Clucking Porridge forward, Alice started to head out towards the dusty path that wound its way around the fields.

"Can you take the lead rein off?" Mia said. "I never got led around in my lessons at Wood Farm."

"That's the name of the riding school in the city," Dominique explained. "I don't know anything

about horses, but Rachel, her instructor, said Mia was a real natural."

Alice thought for a moment and then unclipped the lead rein. She was close enough to grab Porridge if he made a run for it or spied some tasty grass. She had wondered if Dominique was just being a proud mum, but she soon realised that Mia *was* good. Really good. Porridge was lazy by nature and needed quite a lot of riding forward, but already he was in a lovely swinging walk, his head in a soft and natural outline, ears pricked and flicking back and forth as he listened to his young rider. And Alice hadn't seen Mia once kick him or pull on his reins; she was quiet with her aids but effective too. They looked great together.

The path had opened up into one of the paddocks occasionally used for schooling so that the ponies got used to a different surface to the arena.

"Can I trot?" Mia asked, and before Alice could

really think about it Mia had nudged Porridge forward into a rhythmical trot, his strong neck curved into a soft outline, his black mane bouncing as Mia rose and fell to his strides.

Dominique was right: Mia was a natural. She and Porridge looked as though they'd been a partnership for years. Rounding a corner, Mia then sat quietly, bringing her inside leg back slightly and asked Porridge to canter. With a swish of his mane Porridge struck off perfectly on the right leg and cantered beautifully in a circle before Mia steadied him and brought him back to Alice, her eyes sparkling, the biggest grin on her face.

"Sorry!" she said. "It's been months and months since I rode! He's the best."

"My mum should see you ride!" Alice smiled, pleased by the turn in events. She'd expected to lead Porridge around at a sedate walk, but this was something else. Porridge could be tricky

at times and Mia had made him look a million dollars. "Come back tomorrow and have a proper ride in the school."

Mia looked delighted, jumping down from Porridge and hugging Alice tightly. "This is the best day I've had all year!" she grinned, and her enthusiasm was infectious.

For an afternoon Alice had forgotten all about the team and the big competition ahead and just enjoyed the ponies with Mia. Suddenly she couldn't wait until tomorrow!

★

If Alice had been impressed, it was nothing compared to her mum the next afternoon. As Mia trotted and cantered the black Shetland around the arena, Alice glanced at her mum, who was clearly delighted. Porridge was a firm yard favourite, and Alice often felt it was unfair he was missed out because he was too little. When Porridge had qualified for Hickstead, Josephine had been over the moon, and then so disappointed a few weeks later when it was clear his temporary rider's commitments were going to clash. Porridge deserved his moment in the spotlight – he'd been such a loyal pony over the years – and as Alice looked at her mum again, she could almost see the same thoughts running through her mind. She held her breath. Was her mum going to ask?

"Mia," Josephine said slowly, as Mia finished a perfect figure of eight and brought Porridge to a square halt. "How do you feel about doing this regularly? I have an idea…"

★

"I still can't believe it!"

Mia and her mum and Alice and her mum were sitting on a stack of shavings bales in the yard, letting the warm sunshine wash over them. Mia was still chatting away, overflowing

with excitement after Josephine had asked if she wanted to regularly ride Porridge, saying that if they were confident enough as a partnership, Josephine would allow Mia to ride the Shetland in the junior ridden class at the Royal International at Hickstead.

"Are you really sure?" she continued. "I mean, really, really sure?"

Josephine smiled. "Really sure," she said. "The junior is one class we never quite got with Porridge; he did plenty of lead rein with Alice, but she was on her pony Honey for the next few years. He'd love another trip out for old times' sake."

★

With Mia's lesson and all the chatting that went on afterwards it hadn't left Alice very long to get Secret over to Hilltops for team training, so Josephine offered to run the pair over in the lorry. Mia and her mum had finally left, but not before Mia had run back to Porridge's stable several times to hug him!

"That was a good idea." Alice's mum smiled as she carefully eased the big lorry out on to the main road. "Nice to see someone really enjoying the ponies."

Alice agreed. It had been lovely to see Mia's total joy when riding Porridge. They were still chatting happily as they pulled into the yard at Hilltops and Jordan gave them a wave.

"Did the new member join you last time?" Alice's mum asked, waving back as she pulled up next to Jordan's mum's trailer.

"Yep," Alice said, unbuckling her seat belt. "Chloe Williams. She's got a lovely pony."

"Chloe Williams," her mum repeated with a frown. "Her name sounds familiar… I wonder if it's from the ring?"

"She only showjumps, I think," Alice explained.

Leaping down as Secret gave a cheerful whinny from the back, she fastened her hat on. Josephine needed to head home, so after quickly unloading Secret and her tack Alice stood back as her mum slowly turned the enormous lorry in the car park. Eventually, after some careful manoeuvring, Alice's mum was heading back out of the gate, giving a small wave of thanks to the car and trailer that had been waiting to come in, driven by Chloe's dad, who waved in response. He then parked up next to Alice, who was now putting her saddle on, as Chloe climbed out of the passenger seat.

"Hello again," Alice said in what she hoped was a friendly voice, aware her arrival had held Chloe up. "Sorry about that."

Chloe swung her dark ponytail over one shoulder. "Does your mum think *she's* too famous for pony club too?" she said.

Alice was confused. "What?" she said, unsure why Chloe was asking about her mum. "No, she's just busy."

"I suppose the pony club isn't her scene." Chloe had turned back to the trailer now, ready to unload her pony.

Alice blinked. It was no secret that Josephine was a big name in the horse world and often had her results and pictures in *Horse & Hound*. If Alice really thought about it, her mum was probably the most well-known parent in the branch when it came to horses. But there was no need for Chloe to be rude! Amy had said she was really nice. But so far that hadn't been Alice's impression.

Alice tried to put Chloe out of her mind during the lesson. Angus was working on doubles again, and as Secret tended to rush them she needed to concentrate. She knew the course at Hickstead would be technical. Secret had jumped some hard

courses in the past, both at the Festival of the Horse in France and at Olympia, but he'd never been an easy ride. His natural scope and balance got him out of many tricky situations, but Alice had to ride him properly. Secret got himself so overexcited when jumping that it had taken a lot of work to learn to go with his exuberance. For some reason he was unsettled and was making Alice work harder than usual that afternoon. When it came to their turn he was bouncing on the spot, pulling her into the jumps, trying to take off on landing, and Alice was getting flustered. She noticed Chloe watching her carefully as she finally pulled up after a lap of the arena, giving a rueful grin as she patted Secret and rode back to where Angus was standing, one eyebrow raised.

"Well," he said good-naturedly, "been a while since we saw the old Secret!" Then he turned his attention to the group. "I've been thinking about

Hickstead," he continued, "just so we can start to get in the zone. I was thinking, Jordan, you'd jump first. Is that OK?"

Jordan nodded. "Fine with me."

Alice knew that was a good choice. Jordan never seemed to get nervous, and was steady and dependable, and Ziggy, his calm and easy horse, was always on good form. If Jordan jumped clear, then it would get the team off to a good start and raise morale.

"Then Amy, and then Chloe," Angus said, nodding at each team member in turn. "And, Alice, it'll be you jumping last."

Alice bit her lip. She knew why Angus had chosen them; with her previous competition results he needed his strongest pairing at the end to make up any points and beat the clock. It was a huge ask, but an honour too. Who'd have thought she and Secret, once the gossip of pony

club for Secret's hair-raising antics, would now be heading up the pony club team at the most famous showjumping ground in England?

"OK." She smiled. "Happy to do that."

"Good choice!" Amy grinned. "Secret can pick up the slack." She was only half joking, Alice realised, feeling the pressure. But there was something about the way Chloe was looking at her as Amy talked, something more than just dislike. It was real burning resentment. What was going on?

★

"Who's that?" Amy asked as they left the arena after their lesson, and Alice looked at where her friend was pointing. A girl with a familiar face, huge smile and neatly braided hair was waving madly as she perched on the fence.

"Hi, Alice!"

It was Mia! Alice had briefly mentioned she was

heading over to Hilltops to train and had said to Mia she could always come along and watch if she'd wanted. A mountain bike lay discarded in the grass next to her, a cycle helmet dangling from Mia's arm.

"I've been watching you. Secret's so cool!" Mia continued with a grin, jumping down and joining Alice as she rode through the gate.

"Fan club?" Amy grinned. "Angus should start charging for spectators!"

Alice couldn't help but groan inwardly as Chloe rode past wordlessly at that exact moment, shooting Alice and Mia a dirty look. What *was* her problem?

"Ha, ha," she said. "No, this is Mia. She's going to come and help Mum with Porridge, aren't you?"

"Yep!" Mia's eyes were sparkling. "Can I cycle back with you now?"

Alice shrugged. "If you like," she said. "Give

54

me five secs to speak to Angus, then we'll go."

She jumped off Secret and Mia bounded forward, attempting to help and run the stirrup up on the other side but getting the leather in a slight muddle.

"Here," said Alice, pulling the stirrup back down and rearranging it. "Like this, see?"

"Got it!"

Mia was so enthusiastic that Alice let her lead Secret round the yard while she checked in with Angus and confirmed some last details for the entry form.

As she came out of the office she smiled at Secret's bemused expression as Mia led him round diligently, and her heart swelled at the sight of her little red gelding being so gentle with the younger girl. It was as if he knew when he had to really behave.

"Coming, Mia!" she said, waving, and Mia

waved back, dropping the reins, and Secret took advantage of the loosened grip to grab some grass growing underneath the arena fence. Then he trod on the slackened reins. Secret tried to lift his head back up, gave a startled lurch and the reins snapped clean in two. Now free, he just shook his head and resumed his grazing as if nothing had happened.

But Chloe was leading Mac past at that exact moment, and he spooked slightly at the noise and movement.

Chloe glared at Mia. "Watch it!" she hissed.

Mia scowled. "It was an accident!" she responded crossly, then looked at Alice, who had joined her. "I'm so sorry, Alice." She looked downcast. "I didn't mean to."

Taking Secret back, Alice dismissed any irritated feelings about the broken reins. The same thing had happened to her in the past.

"It's fine," she said. "They were old reins, and I'm sure Hannah will lend me some for riding home." She smiled. "Come on, let's go."

Mia grinned in relief and headed off to find her bike.

Chloe raised an eyebrow after the younger girl was out of earshot. "Surprised your mum allows her near your precious horses."

Alice frowned. "What do you mean by that?" she said defensively.

But Chloe smiled sweetly. "Just an observation."

And she was off before Alice could think of a retort. She shook her head instead. She couldn't work Chloe out at all!

Chapter 5

In the days that followed, Mia often accompanied Alice on her bike back over the downs – pushing the bike up the steepest bits, freewheeling down the hills, all the while chatting nineteen to the dozen – and it soon felt as though she was a permanent part of the yard. The school summer holidays had just begun and every day the familiar sight of a mountain bike being pushed up the drive – and

the crescendo of whinnies from the ponies who all adored Mia – never failed to make Alice smile.

Secret and Porridge remained Mia's firm favourites, and Alice could tell her pony liked Mia a lot. There was no better judge of character than Secret! He even let Mia catch him in from the field, something only Alice could usually do. However, Alice had quickly realised that although Mia was a naturally gifted rider, she'd never had the chance to learn any sort of stable management. Mia had to be shown everything, from mucking out to filling a hay net, even the right way to put a head collar on. And yet with no Finn to chat to and long days looking after the horses, Alice found that it was really rewarding showing Mia how to carry out the most basic of tasks, especially as she was such good company.

As they carried the last two water buckets over to the furthest stable – Porridge's – Mia stretched her arms wide.

"I think my arms have grown a metre carrying all those. Why do you carry the buckets over just to carry them back again when they're full?" she asked, and Alice had to stop and think.

"I don't know!" she replied. "We just always have."

"Why don't you take the hose to the bucket?" Mia giggled, and Alice looked at her, before she shook her head and smiled.

"Do you know, I've never even thought about it." She couldn't believe she'd been making work harder for herself. "Let's do it your way next time!"

Mia laughed. "Bet you're glad I'm here. What did you do before I came along?"

There was an infectious side to Mia's personality, and Alice always felt more cheerful in her company.

Alice's mum seemed to be enjoying herself too. Although she had clients' ponies to prepare for

the summer shows, when their owners or their owner's children rode them, it was never quite the same as having one of the yard favourites out and about. With Porridge now entered for the Royal International at Hickstead with Mia as his rider, preparing the little Shetland and Mia had given Alice's mum a new focus. She and Mia spent hours watching past videos of junior classes before practising their show in the arena.

Alice had dug out her old showing kit, allowing herself a few moments of nostalgia as she held the pink ties, the hair ribbons and the canary yellow jodhpurs that had once been her uniform. *These old jacket and jodhs should fit Mia*, she thought, holding them up. And she was right. The jacket was slightly long in the arm, and Mia needed to wear one of her school shirts, but with a belt on the jodhpurs and jodhpur clips over her conker-brown boots, Mia looked perfect.

Twirling around in front of the mirror in Alice's bedroom Mia grinned. "I've always dreamed of wearing all this," she said happily, inspecting her reflection once again. "My old instructor would go crazy if she saw me now!"

"Do you miss your old stables?" Alice wanted to find out more about Mia's path into ponies.

Mia nodded. "Loads," she said slightly wistfully. "Where I lived before..." She frowned. "It was the one good thing, let's just say that. It wasn't a nice area. I thought I'd never ride again when we moved; I didn't know how to get to know anyone horsey! But then you and your mum said I could come up here, and it's better than ever before! My mum doesn't know where I got my love of horses from. She says 'horse' was my first word!"

"Some people are just born horse lovers," Alice smiled. "You're one of them."

Mia glanced up at the string of rosettes bordering Alice's ceiling and the photos of Secret everywhere. "Do you think you'd still ride if your mum wasn't horsey?" she asked, and Alice paused before answering.

Riding Secret, that was when she felt most alive, felt confident, felt as though she could do anything.

"I'd hope so," she said.

Mia smiled. "Come on," she said happily. "Fergus told me he's got cake today. Race you out to the stables!"

Laughing, Alice followed Mia out into the yard, the heat hitting her and a chorus of whinnies greeting the girls. With Mia coming to Hickstead, the Hilltops branch entered for the showjumping and pony club camp to look forward to before the big show, the summer holidays were looking the best ever, Alice thought, even without Finn around. She really missed him, but with Mia around the yard most days, the stables were a happy place to be.

★

Amy was full of excited chatter next time Alice and Secret headed over to Hilltops. As Secret rolled in the little paddock after the lesson, Alice sat in the cool of the café, sipping on a cold drink as she pulled her damp pale hair back into a ponytail.

"So, big news," Amy said in a gossipy voice, pulling out her phone. "You've heard of Dupont Equestrian, haven't you?"

Alice nodded. They were a company who made the most gorgeous jumping jackets and boots and matching saddlecloths. They also made the blue stirrups that Alice had wanted for ages and which she had finally been able to buy with the money she received from Secret's photo, which had been used in a high-end fashion magazine

following their French adventure. She treasured them. She'd pored over the rest of the products at Olympia, vowing to one day kit Secret out in all their gear when they could afford the eye-wateringly expensive prices.

"Yes?" Alice said in a puzzled voice, wondering what Amy was about to say. Her friend was looking incredibly excited, even for her. "They make my dream stirrups, remember?!"

"Sooooo," Amy grinned, as if trying to prolong the suspense, "I might have had a little message from their PR lady. It turns out she's noticed those blue stirrups in Secret's photos!"

"OK...?" Alice said slowly.

"So, get this," Amy continued. "They know about you going to Hickstead and they want to kit you out! From head to toe, or hoof really, as they want to kit Secret out too. Isn't that just the coolest? You need to talk to your mum; she'll have to take it from here if she agrees."

For a few seconds Alice didn't know what to say. "You're joking?" she said, feeling a smile break out. "That's amazing!"

But something felt off. Amy had only mentioned her and Secret. "You'll get stuff as well, right?" she asked. "The rest of the team?"

Amy snorted with laughter. "No, silly!" she said good-naturedly. "It's you and Secret who are the stars." She grinned. "And anyway, you don't get a choice. I already replied saying yes, you'd love to." Then she looked up and waved. "Hey, Chloe, over here!"

Glancing over, Alice saw Chloe approach their sofa.

"You OK?" Amy asked in a friendly voice, budging over so there was room for her. "Look, check this out."

And Amy showed Chloe the screen, pointing

out the gorgeous jacket, boots and all the horsey kit Dupont Equestrian were planning to send Alice in exchange for publicity. It turned out that they also wanted to come over themselves to photograph Alice and Secret in the kit soon if her mum agreed. She groaned inwardly – she hated posing for photos – but it was a brilliant offer. It's just there was so much to concentrate on right now, what with camp and Hickstead coming up. Still, she'd fit it in somehow. And Amy was right: it *was* pretty cool!

"Amazing, huh?" Amy grinned.

Chloe smiled thinly. "If you like that sort of thing," she said coolly. "It's rather flash for me."

"I know, it is a bit," Amy said cheerfully, not picking up on Chloe's tone. "Alice, you have to jump well at Hickstead now with all this new gear!"

"Yes, can't let your *fans* down," Chloe added,

and Amy giggled.

Alice smiled too, but she was feeling uncomfortable. It felt as though every time she was near Chloe, Secret's fame was brought up, and Alice felt that Chloe had made up her mind about her already.

★

At least Mia, with her enthusiasm and endless love for the ponies on the yard, provided a happy distraction for whatever Chloe seemed to have against Alice. Although sometimes Alice felt like she was imagining it. Jordan and Amy seemed to get along with Chloe just fine; in fact, Amy had told Alice they'd all been out to the cinema and had a really fun time.

"Did she … um…" Alice hadn't quite known how to phrase it. "Did she say anything about me?"

Amy had looked at her in amazement before

bursting into laughter. "What?" she'd chuckled. "No! Why would she?"

"Oh," Alice had said, feeling more confused than ever. "No reason."

She and Chloe continued to ignore each other during training. Alice noticed she always positioned her dapple-grey pony on the other end of the line-up to Alice, standing next to Jordan's or Amy's pony instead. Alice had tried to engage Chloe in conversation a few times in the café afterwards, but Chloe always answered her in words of one syllable, before turning back to Jordan and Amy. Alice had given up. She couldn't *make* someone like her. But with camp, the highlight of the pony club calendar coming up next week, she hoped they would soon get on better.

Chapter 6

It wasn't only Josephine and Alice who had noticed Mia's enthusiasm for helping around the yard. Angus, visiting one afternoon, had been equally charmed by Mia as she proudly showed him how she was able to lead in Ella from the field.

"Well done!" Angus smiled as Mia led the grey mare towards her stable and he opened the door in readiness.

"Not yet!" Mia had said firmly. "I need to pick out her feet and check her legs first." She tied Ella up and ran a hand down her leg, gently instructing the mare to pick up a front foot. "Like this, see?"

"Great job!" Angus looked impressed, then thoughtful. "We had a member drop out of camp next week… How old are you, Mia?"

"Ten, eleven next month," Mia answered proudly. "I start senior school in September."

Angus smiled. "That should be fine. If I talked to your mum and she says it's fine, what do you say to joining us at camp, in the juniors? It's three days of lessons at Hilltops, but lots of fun stuff as well, rides out, games and things. You'd love it."

Mia grinned. "A-mazing!" she replied, and Josephine, who had joined them, nodded in agreement.

"Porridge would love it too," she said. "And it would keep him refreshed for Hickstead. Great idea, Angus! Mia, I'll talk to your mum."

"If it means I'm out from under Mum's feet during the summer holidays, she'll be all for it," Mia said. "She works shifts, though, so getting me over might be a problem." She frowned, suddenly not looking too sure.

"Don't worry about anything," Alice's mum said kindly. "We'll make sure you get to where you need to every day."

Mia perked up. "Thanks, Mrs Smalley!"

Alice's mum waved a hand dismissively. "Call me Josephine, and it's fine, honestly!"

Alice watched the exchange, happy that Mia was also going to get to experience pony club camp. She couldn't wait either! Alice had heard so much about it but not yet taken part due to being in France the summer before. They could look out for each other! And her mum seemed happy too. Josephine had a reputation in the showing

world as being a bit of an ice queen, but just like when Ella had arrived on the yard, Mia's presence seemed to have brought out a softer side to her.

"To camp then!" Mia grinned.

Alice gave her a thumbs up. "Can't wait!"

★

Dupont Equestrian had been in contact with Alice's mum about kitting Alice and Secret out for Hickstead. Alice wasn't going to be paid, but the prestigious company were going to send her all their latest clothes and equipment in exchange for a one-off double-page advert in *Horse & Hound*.

"Jo from Dupont rang," Alice's mum said one evening as they finished off the water buckets. "She agreed that during the second day of camp they'll come over and shoot at Hilltops. While you're over there anyway it makes sense to use their big arena, and you can use the showjumps. Angus is happy for it to go ahead."

"I thought it was just going to be Secret and me at home?" Alice said, suddenly feeling unsure. This was turning into a bigger deal than she'd anticipated.

"Well," her mum replied, "when they heard you had camp, they came up with another idea. Jo has assured me it shouldn't take too long." Her mum stopped and smiled at her. "I'm sure no one will mind – it's exciting!"

But Alice had started to feel uneasy. It was a big enough deal being sent all the gorgeous kit, but now she had to have her photograph taken in front of the whole pony club…

★

"Oh, don't worry about that!" Amy laughed when Alice told her about her concerns a few days later. "I can help you get Secret ready. It'll be fun. Everyone will love it!"

"OK, if you're sure…" Alice agreed reluctantly.

Although she'd rather have had the photo shoot at home, with no one else watching, it *was* all quite exciting, and she couldn't wait to see the beautiful things Dupont were going to send her. She just hoped her mum and Amy were right and the rest of the camp members didn't mind their morning being disrupted.

"I put a photo of Secret up online, announcing there would be some exciting news this week," Amy then said, and Alice drew out her phone so she could read Amy's latest post. There were already loads of messages complimenting Secret on being the cutest pony ever, wishing him luck for camp, some asking how his Hickstead prep was going. Scrolling down, Alice stopped in her tracks, feeling herself go hot and cold. There was one message that stood out from the others, the words burning in Alice's head as she read them.

Must be so easy when Mummy buys the best ponies

and all you have to do is sit there.

The words were Alice's weakness, her Achilles heel. She knew how lucky she was. But she'd been desperate to prove herself with Secret, a pony she'd trained on her own, and she'd suffered some humiliating moments along the way in public. Secret was far from a ready-made pony, even if he looked it to an outsider.

"Who sent this message?" Alice showed the phone to Amy.

Amy paused for a second too long. "Oh, it's just from some made-up name. Don't worry about it!" she said dismissively. "You're bound to get some strange messages from time to time."

"Yes, but…" Alice tried to think about how to say that this particular message was targeting her biggest riding fear, that people thought she was just jumping another pony of her mum's, that she wasn't actually that good a rider. "It's

quite *personal*."

Amy shrugged. "Well, your mum's well known, I guess? Don't worry about it."

But Alice wasn't going to let it drop. "Have you had other messages like this?"

"It's literally just one or two out of *thousands*," Amy said in a cheerful voice. "Probably just sour grapes."

"I don't like it," Alice mumbled. "And what if I do badly at Hickstead? What awful things might people say then?"

Amy laughed. "Well, for a start, you won't," she said confidently. "And, secondly, don't worry! If you weren't so well known, you wouldn't be getting opportunities like these freebies from Dupont. Just ignore them! I bet even Charlotte Dujardin gets weird messages now and again."

"I guess, but…" Alice's voice trailed off.

Amy seemed entirely unconcerned. But Alice

couldn't help but feel as though there was one major difference between her and famous riders. They had known by going into their careers they'd be in the public eye, and they had whole teams of people around them to help and support and advise them.

Alice and Secret's journey had been entirely unexpected. For a start he was more talented than Alice had ever dreamed of when she'd first been given the mischievous colt, and a lot of his appeal was his personality and bravery during situations Alice had been unwittingly dragged into, such as his wrongful kidnapping in London over Christmas. All Alice had ever wanted was just to be the best she could be with her beloved red pony; everything else had come as a bonus. But was it a bonus? Sure, she was looking forward to receiving the Dupont goodies, but the messages had left her feeling vulnerable.

Chapter 7

Two ponies, two riders, and three days of camp ahead made for quite a lot of organisation at Park Farm!

"Is it actually camping?" Mia had asked as they returned from a hack late one afternoon.

"No," Alice explained. "It's three days of lessons in the same place. I think some members *are* camping there overnight, but we'll hack over every morning."

Both Porridge and Secret had a stable allocated to them for daytime use, then they'd hack back each evening so the two ponies could enjoy some downtime in their own fields at home. Then Alice and Mia could return for the non-riding evening activities, such as swimming and the barbecue.

★

Both girls were full of chatter as they tacked up in the yard at Park Farm. Mia had cycled over early, and the sun was already warming the cobbles of the yard, the ponies swishing tails against flies as Fergus led them in, three at a time, from the dew-soaked paddocks, ready to enjoy the cool of their stables. Mia's mum had sent her over with two of the pony club-branded polo shirts and Alice had dug out some more of her outgrown jodhpurs. Alice's mum was going to drive over to Hilltops and leave all the gear they'd need for

the day: Secret's jumping boots, their lunchboxes, cooler rugs for in between lessons. As they swung themselves up into the saddles, Porridge gave his thick forelock a swish, as if mirroring his young rider's excitement and Alice smiled, clucking at Secret to lead the way over the downs towards Hilltops.

"This is the best thing that's ever happened to me." Mia and Porridge jogged happily alongside Secret as the chalky path opened up on to the rolling hill, Alice's favourite bit of the ride. Rabbits lay sunning themselves on the open grass, seemingly unbothered by the oncoming horses, and a few sheep headed slowly for the more wooded areas to settle themselves down in the shade.

"When I lived in the city, I always wanted to hack out," Mia continued. "But it got really busy around the stables, so we just rode in the school."

"The riding school sounds like a brilliant place,

though," Alice said, thinking how amazing it was that Mia had been able to learn to ride in the middle of a big city. And they'd obviously done a great job of teaching her.

"Yeah, it was," Mia said. "I miss it. My friend said when we moved out here all the horse people would be really snobby. I told a girl at my school about your mum, cos we both love Secret, and she couldn't believe it." She shrugged. "She said she didn't think your mum would let anyone ride her ponies."

Alice frowned, thinking back to Chloe's words, which had almost mirrored those.

"But she's so nice!" Mia continued before Alice could say anything. "I told my friend she was totally wrong."

"Well," Alice replied, "Mum lives for the ponies, and her business is really important. So she's always been quite choosy about who can come up

to the yard."

They'd almost reached Hilltops now, and the yard was bustling with activity. There were around twenty pony club members taking part. Alice and Mia would be in separate groups during the day, as Alice was older and more experienced and would be with Jordan, Amy and Hannah.

"I'll take you to meet June; she's the district commissioner," Alice explained to Mia. "She's sort of like the head teacher of pony club. She can come across as being a bit scary but she's actually really nice."

"Got it!" Mia grinned.

Once Alice had found June and Mia's group instructor, a smiley lady called Erica, Alice went to find her group. Her pony club friends would all be there, Holly and Sam who she'd been to France with, Amy, Jordan, Lola and Hannah, and Chloe. Chloe nodded coolly at Alice, and Alice nodded back, feeling as awkward as ever in her company. She kept quiet when Chloe was around because everything she said seemed to be taken the wrong way.

Angus was going to lead the jumping sessions, but the group were also going to have flatwork and dressage sessions with visiting instructors. Alice knew she was going to have to work hard to get Secret to concentrate during those. Flatwork was a huge part of jumping, but Secret associated Hilltops with coloured poles and tended to get overexcited. Still, it would be nothing compared to his excitement on the final day! The senior members were going to have the chance to ride over a cross-country course in the fields surrounding Hilltops. Part of the ride crossed the open downs Alice regularly hacked across. Secret was an amazing jumper, but Alice had never done anything like it before with him and, although

she was looking forward to the ride, she had a knot in her tummy every time she thought about it. They'd no longer have the fence of an arena to contain Secret's excitement; he'd be galloping and jumping across the open countryside! It was so far out of her comfort zone.

"Hey, Alice!" Jordan interrupted her thoughts as they waited in the arena for an instructor. Angus had arranged for a dressage rider to take the first session. "Amy told me about the Dupont deal – fancy!" He grinned. "I'm pretty jealous, I've got to admit. Do you know how much that stuff costs?"

Everyone turned to look at Alice and she felt herself redden slightly. "Yeah, I know. It's amazing," she replied quietly.

"I'll say!" Sam, on Jordan's other side, chimed in.

"Any chance you could nab us some freebies?" Jordan smiled.

"OK, quiet please!" A man dressed in smart khaki breeches and shiny boots strode into the middle of the group. "Enough chit-chatting."

Chloe glanced at Alice and narrowed her eyes. "Sorry," she said sweetly. "Alice was telling us all about the shoot tomorrow."

The instructor folded his arms. "Well, I'm not interested," he said. "I'm here for two hours only and I want to see your best work. So can we now concentrate on riding?" He looked pointedly at Alice as he said this.

Everyone immediately fell silent.

Great, Alice thought. Now, thanks to Chloe, she'd made a bad impression on the dressage instructor. She felt herself redden once again, annoyed that *she'd* been blamed for other people chatting about the photo shoot!

When Chloe passed by her on her dapple-grey pony she gave Alice a small smile. But it wasn't

a friendly smile. It was one that said, *Ha, you deserved that.*

★

The lesson improved after that, and Alice hoped the instructor had been impressed with the group's work, and in particular her and Secret. Secret had an extravagant movement and his Welsh paces, inherited from his beautiful dam Lily, were showstopping. As Alice carried out a ten-metre circle in canter, she had grinned, enjoying the huge power in her small pony. After initially putting his ears back in disgust and pulling a furious expression when he'd realised there was to be no jumping, he'd settled down and really listened to Alice, earning a couple of 'well done's. But now she was more than ready for a break!

★

"Alice, over here!"

Alice gave Secret a pat as she led him to his day

stable. She was thinking about Chloe. She knew Chloe had tried to get her in trouble deliberately, but why?

"Hey, Mia." Alice joined her friend as Mia dismounted from Porridge after coming back from the riding field. Another younger girl – a junior pony clubber leading a bay pony – nudged Mia and said something Alice couldn't hear.

"Yeah!" Mia grinned at her new friend. "I told you: she's really nice!" Turning to Alice, her eyes sparkled. "No one believed me when I said I was riding your pony!"

"I-I follow your pony Secret," the young girl stammered. "He's so cool!"

"Er, thanks!" Alice felt disconcerted. "He is, yes!" Then she couldn't think of anything else to say.

Settling down with Mia on the grass once she'd helped put Porridge away, Alice stretched,

enjoying the warmth of the sun. They had jumping that afternoon, and she couldn't wait. Amy, Lola and Hannah joined Alice and Mia. They all attacked their picnic lunches with gusto, hungry after their lessons. Mia chatted away, telling Alice how she and Porridge had been doing pole exercises and how much she'd learnt. Their conversation was interrupted as a big black van drove slowly into the yard, before a young man hopped out with a clipboard.

"I'm looking for Alice Smalley," he called, as Angus approached asking if he could help. Everyone turned to stare at Alice. "Delivery?"

"Oooh," Amy said. "This must be the Dupont stuff!"

Alice climbed to her feet as the man unloaded two big boxes from the back of the van.

Alice and her friends carried the boxes over to the stable area and Amy used a hoof pick to tear open the boxes. "Wow!" she said as she pulled out the most exquisitely cut cobalt-blue jacket. "This is gorgeous!"

It seemed to Alice as though she had been sent the entire Dupont range. The softest breeches, a riding belt with a diamante clasp and the most beautiful long boots Alice had ever seen, which were made from butter-soft leather. As she slipped them on over her old navy jodhs they seemed to elongate her already long legs, making her stand taller and straighter. Secret had done well too. A gorgeous saddlecloth, a rug that was trimmed in the same cobalt blue and matching leg wraps. It was all going to look amazing against the red of his coat, Alice thought, feeling a sudden thrill of excitement and pushing the horrid message from the day before to the back of her mind. Even the thought of the photo shoot in front of everyone now didn't feel so bad.

A PONY called SECRET

"So gorgeous!" Mia held up the saddlecloth, the diamantes sewn into the trim sparkling in the hot sun. "You *are* lucky, Alice!"

By now everyone had gathered round to see what was going on. Mia was in her element, giggling with her new friends, showing them the contents of the boxes and modelling the different items. Glancing up, Alice noticed Chloe raise an eyebrow, her nose wrinkled. But caught up in the excitement, Alice tried to ignore her. Chloe obviously had a problem with her, but she wasn't going to let it worry her!

Chapter 8

Secret had never felt better in his afternoon jumping session. The intensive dressage lesson had taken the edge off his exuberance, but he remained as energetic as ever, light and supple in Alice's hands, but as though he could jump the moon. Angus was in a challenging mood and yet every time he raised the poles on the jumps it posed no problem for Secret. Alice felt the hot air

whip through her ponytail as Secret cleared fence after fence, landing in perfect harmony with her, and in one fluid movement seeming to twist his body to face the next jump. For the few moments she was jumping, as always, Alice felt as though it was just her and Secret.

"Fantastic." Angus gave a satisfied grin. "No more jumping in an arena for the rest of the week, until the show warm-up. He's going so well that we don't want to push it. Let's enjoy the rest of camp, and then think about Hickstead."

Alice nodded, giving Secret his reins, allowing the little gelding to stretch his head long and low. Angus was right. Secret didn't need to be over-jumped. She rarely jumped him at home, only during their lessons, and hacked the rest of the time to keep him sharp and fit. It was a routine that suited him.

"We'll be counting on you, Alice!" Jordan, next

to her grinned. "Last rider to go and everything."

Alice grimaced. "Don't remind me!"

"Oh, I'm sure Secret the wonder pony will save the day if needed."

It was Chloe, next to Jordan, who said this with a little smile. It sounded as though she was being complimentary, but Alice recognised the sarcastic tone.

Alice was getting fed up with it now. "Let's hope so," she said in a bland voice. She wasn't going to rise to Chloe's little digs, even if she seemed to be the only one who noticed them.

★

"How was your day?"

It was a beautiful evening, and Mia and Alice were taking their time as they hacked their ponies home later.

"Awesome!" Mia grinned, giving Porridge a quick hug. "Porridge behaved so well. We had

games in the afternoon. Everyone was talking about your photo shoot tomorrow. *All* of us juniors are coming to watch!"

Alice gulped. "Great!" was all she could say.

Mia frowned. "I'm a bit nervous about one thing tomorrow, though – we're swapping ponies," she explained. "I know I've ridden Porridge lots, but I'm worried about getting on a bigger pony and having to adjust the tack and stuff."

Alice was just about to say it didn't matter, that she was sure someone would help her when she saw Mia's face. She could tell it meant a lot to Mia to give the right impression in front of her new friends. Alice remembered how she'd felt at the same age. "Hmmm," she said instead. "Let's have a quick practice now."

Secret was relaxed after the long day at pony club, meandering along on the familiar route home. If there was ever a time for Mia to have a quick sit on him, it was now.

"On Secret?" Mia said in wonder.

Alice shrugged. "Why not?" she said. "The pony you ride tomorrow will probably be more or less the same size. I think Porridge is the only Shetland at camp."

Hopping down as Mia jumped lightly off Porridge, Alice handed the reins over.

"See, like this," she said, as Mia swung herself up in the saddle. "Push your leg back and get the stirrup bar. You'll need to put them up a few holes for your height." And Alice showed Mia exactly what she should do when she got on the strange pony, how to adjust the stirrups, to check what sort of bridle the pony had on, the things she had to look out for when getting on a different pony for the first time.

Mia nodded, listening intently. "Thank you," she smiled. "Shall I get off now?"

Alice looked at Secret, who was gazing down the valley at Park Farm, a speck in the distance. His eyes were soft, his ears pricked.

"Why don't you ride him the rest of the way home? Get yourself really ready for pony swapping tomorrow!" she suggested, taking Porridge's reins over his head to lead him home. Porridge tossed his thick black mane, impatient to get back to his pony nuts and hay net.

"Wowee!" Mia grinned. "I'm actually riding Redgrove Secret! Somebody pinch me!"

Alice chuckled. And as Mia nudged the little red pony on and he set off with a beautiful swinging walk, she was once again struck by Mia's natural position and soft hands. Secret obviously liked her. Alice remembered the time a boy called Seb had ridden Secret in France and the gelding had hated him straight away. It had been awful. But as Mia, at Alice's suggestion, nudged Secret into a trot up

97

the last stretch of turf, it was as though Secret was smiling. They were in total sync together.

The second day of camp dawned sunny and beautiful. So Secret looked his best for the photo shoot, Fergus was going to box Porridge and Secret over to Hilltops. Alice and Mia had given Secret a bath the night before, and his red coat sparkled, his mane and tail silken strands. His tack was polished and Alice had washed her own hair with extra care. She still couldn't decide how to wear it. In some sort of elaborate French plait? Or a long ponytail like her hero Devon Jenkins? She wondered if she'd see Devon at Hickstead, which was only a few days away now.

Mia, giving one of her own black braids a tug, waved her hands in front of Alice's face as she sat next to her in the cab. "Earth to Alice!" she grinned, and Alice gave a start and smiled.

"Sorry!" she said. "Just thinking about stuff. Hickstead actually. What with camp and everything I keep forgetting it's so close."

"Chloe is in your team, isn't she? She's not very nice, is she?" Mia said casually, and Alice turned to her, startled. "Did you know her or something before she joined pony club?"

Alice shook her head. "No," she said. "I might have seen her at shows, but that's it. When did you meet her?"

"I said hello when I was in the tack room yesterday," Mia explained. "She was looking for something so I started chatting and told her I was riding Porridge. I said he was your mum's Shetland pony. She made a face and gave me a really horrible look, then stomped off. So weird!"

Alice shrugged. "She just seems to have it in for me," she confided. "I honestly don't know why."

"Do you think she wrote those messages?" Mia

added and Alice frowned, looking across at her friend.

"What messages?" she said in a worried voice.

Mia chewed on her lip. "I heard Amy talking to that boy on your team, Jordan? Amy was saying she was having to delete more and more mean messages."

Alice felt the sharp sting of humiliation as she thought back to the words she'd read the other day. The message had left her feeling vulnerable. And now there were more. But they'd arrived at Hilltops now and Mia darted out of the box at once, eager to see her friends, and Alice and Secret needed to get ready for the Dupont crew.

Alice's mum was out judging at a summer show, so her dad was coming to oversee the shoot once he'd finished up his work at home. Amy had promised to help Alice get ready. She was bouncing all over the place with excitement, dragging Alice

along to the tack room where the boxes of clothing and horse equipment were waiting.

"I'll tack Secret up," she said bossily. "You go and get changed."

Doing as she was instructed, Alice wriggled into the breeches and jacket, smoothing down her shirt and attaching a gorgeous horseshoe tiepin, zipping up the soft leather boots and gathering her hair into a bun. Examining herself in the smudged tack-room mirror she allowed herself a little moment of pride. Getting to the top was all about her riding, she knew that, but at that moment she really *felt* the part. She looked like the showjumpers she so admired from the pages of her pony magazines. She felt grown-up, confident and fearless, a world apart from her slightly awkward and shy self. She felt like she could do anything!

Secret looked amazing too. The new saddlecloth and his smart jumping boots made him look like a pony you'd see jumping on television. He was bright-eyed as he pawed the ground, as if in anticipation of being the centre of attention. Secret adored the camera. He only had to see one to put his ears forward and pose, and Alice knew he was going to enjoy the day. And so was she!

"You look fantastic, both of you," a familiar voice said admiringly, and Alice smiled as her dad got out of his car. She was so pleased her dad was there! He might not be horsey but he always supported her.

The Dupont team pulled up into the yard in a sleek black car and Jo, the lady who had been chatting with Alice's mum, introduced herself as the camera crew unloaded their equipment.

Standing back, Jo admired Alice's and Secret's outfits. "This is all going to look fantastic. As I said to your mum on the phone we're looking at a big advert in *Horse & Hound*, but we'll make sure we

drum up lots of publicity over the next few days. Sound OK?"

Alice nodded. "OK," she croaked.

Soon Jo was organising everyone. There was a double set up in the arena that Alice was going to jump a few times, so the team could get the perfect shot. The rest of the pony clubbers, both junior and senior, had started to gather around to watch.

Trotting round, Alice warmed Secret up. Catching a glimpse of her reflection in the arena mirror she felt a smile break through. Secret was beautifully rounded, carrying himself forward in a natural outline, his red mane and tail streaming behind him. The photos were going to look amazing, she thought.

"OK!" Jo called. "When you're ready. We'd like quite a few shots of the jump from different angles, if that's OK. Let's get a couple of warm-ups under our belt, just to test the lighting."

This was it, their big moment. Alice pushed Secret into canter before popping over a couple of smaller cross poles. Then rounding the corner into the double, Alice steadied Secret, sitting deep into the saddle. His rocking horse canter lengthened, his ears pricked forward, and he headed straight for the centre of the jump. He'd never felt better.

Soaring over the double, Alice was aware of cameras clicking, and she hoped she'd folded into a perfect position. Secret had jumped smoothly over in one stride and was over the next in almost one fluid motion.

"Great!" Jo called. "Now let's try another angle." She gestured to the photographer. "Can you go again?" she said to Alice.

Nodding, Alice gathered up the reins and nudged Secret back into canter, rounding the corner again. His ears pricked; he was more than

ready to go again.

Suddenly there was a loud hiss and water poured into the arena. Alice had no time to react; it felt as though she'd jumped into a swimming pool. All at once she was lurching over Secret's neck, grasping his sodden mane as she tried to cling on while the little gelding veered to the side, totally spooked. Too late. She was falling and landed in the soft sand of the arena, now soaked by the jets of water.

"What the—" Sitting up, and realising with relief that Secret was fine and had gone to join the pony clubbers gathered on the fence, Alice blinked, aware of Jo running towards her, a look of shock on her face.

The water was still pumping out from the side of the arena as Hannah's dad, who owned the centre, came over. "It's the arena sprinklers!" He held up his hands. "They're timed to come on at night to reduce dust. I've no idea why they're on now!"

Alice stood up, brushing her breeches and jacket, but it was no good – the mixture of wet dust and dark sand had ruined the new outfit. She was totally unhurt, but the clothes were filthy.

Mia, quickest to react, had jumped off the fence and caught Secret, leading him back to Alice. Everyone else was staring, some looking totally shocked, others whispering to each other. And then there was Chloe right at the end, perched on the rails with a smirk on her face.

Realising Alice was unhurt, Jo now just looked annoyed. "Well," she said snappily, "that wasn't part of the plan, was it?"

"I'm sorry," Alice mumbled. "I couldn't stay on."

"The clothes are totally ruined now," Jo continued frostily. "We'll have to abandon the shoot."

"None of this was Alice's fault!" Her dad said

sharply, joining Jo and Alice. "It's a good thing Secret didn't go completely bonkers!" He put an arm round Alice. "Well done," he said in a quieter voice. "Even *I* know you managed that very well."

Hannah's dad came over scratching his head. "I've no idea how that happened!" he said in a puzzled voice. "I just checked the settings in the tack room, and they'd reset themselves. I'm so sorry."

Alice put her arms round Secret. It wasn't his fault he'd spooked. As well as the pony clubbers, some of Hilltops' livery owners had now gathered round the arena to see what was causing all the commotion. Alice could feel her cheeks burning with embarrassment.

The camera crew were crossly gathering their things. Luckily their expensive equipment had largely escaped damage; it was Alice and Secret who'd received the worst drenching.

Jo sighed heavily. "We had a lot riding on this shoot. We've got a few photos, but only a fraction of what we'd wanted." She pushed her sunglasses back up on her head and smiled thinly. "Not *exactly* a success. I'll be in touch."

Watching her climb back into the sleek black car with the rest of the team, Alice felt her shoulders slump. Talk about a reality check! And now this would be the gossip of camp. A few members were giggling, and the buzz of chatter rang in Alice's ears as she led Secret back to the yard, ready to change back into her trusted navy jodhs and pony club T-shirt.

Chloe passed her on her dapple grey. Looking down at her as she trudged on, Chloe started to giggle.

"That's it," Alice snapped furiously. "Have a good laugh, why don't you?"

Chloe snorted. "Oh, come on! That *was* funny,

you have to admit. And it's not like you're hurt."

Alice glared at her teammate. "No," she replied. "I'm not hurt. But I don't appreciate you being so horrible about it."

Secret placed his head on Alice's shoulder as if in silent solidarity, as Chloe rolled her eyes and rode on. It didn't even matter that Secret had slobbered all over the shoulder of the beautiful jacket, given it would need dry cleaning anyway. Alice gave him a hug.

Once both she and Secret were dry and changed, and her dad had headed off, Alice re-joined her group. She just wanted to concentrate on her lesson and forget everything that had happened that morning!

★

Later that day, after a good lesson, Alice put Secret into his day stable and headed over to the barn where her group were having a talk on veterinary matters. The vet wasn't there yet so they had a few moments to mill around in the sunshine. Mia's junior group were in the outdoor school. Alice didn't want to put off Mia by openly watching her, so she hung back as Mia trotted round on a pretty liver chestnut. She looked totally at home on the new pony. Porridge was enjoying a brief rest, tied up in the shade under the trees at the end of the arena as Mia nudged the pony into a perfect canter. She really was a lovely rider.

"Well done, Mia!" the young instructor called. "Now next time round, go over the cross pole and then the spread."

With a determined look on her face Mia cantered a beautiful circle, turning down into the cross pole. Alice felt herself jump alongside Mia as her friend sat up straight until the last second before folding neatly over the chestnut's neck, her hands soft and yielding as the pony jumped neatly.

On and round to the spread and Alice could see the pony was a little spooked by the bright fillers underneath the jump. She held her breath, but saw the determined nudge of Mia's heel and saw her speak encouragingly to the pony. The two of them sailed over the spooky spread. Mia grinned and patted the pony again and again as they came to a stop next to the instructor.

"Well ridden!" the instructor praised her. "I could see you had to work at the second jump."

And, as Mia rode back to her place in the line, Alice smiled and returned to her group. After such a disastrous morning, it had really cheered her up to see her friend enjoy her riding so much. Mia coming to the yard had been the best thing to happen that summer!

★

At lunchtime Alice was aware of covert glances and whispered giggles as she sat down with her picnic. Amy sat down next to her, looking strangely jumpy.

"What's up?" Alice found she wasn't really hungry for once, and Amy bit her lip.

"Look, try not to be upset," she said. "There's a photo going around. I mean, it's silly…"

Feeling her heart sink, Alice pulled out her phone, and clicked on a photo she'd been tagged in. There she was sitting on the damp sand, her face bright red and hair soaking wet as Secret trotted away.

Oops, not so perfect now! the comment read. The writer was anonymous, but it was obvious to Alice who had written it.

"I bet it was Chloe who uploaded that." Mia, joining Alice, put her head over Alice's shoulder to look at the photo.

Amy looked puzzled. "Chloe?" she said in a bewildered voice. "Why would Chloe do that?"

"Because she doesn't like me," Alice said flatly. "She never has."

"There she is!" Mia leapt to her feet as Chloe stalked across the yard, and ran over to her. "Chloe!" Mia called, her voice angry. "I want a word with you!"

Chloe turned and raised an eyebrow as Alice scrambled to her feet and joined Mia, followed by Amy, who was still looking confused. Alice had been calm up to then, but seeing the smug look on Chloe's face ignited something in her. How dare Chloe post that photo!

"What do you want?" Chloe sounded bored.

"Did you post this photo?" Alice said hotly, holding out her phone.

"We know you did," Mia piped up next to her. "You're just a jealous, horrible person!"

Chloe laughed unkindly. "What's it to you?" she said.

113

"What *is* your problem?" Mia continued. "I've seen how you are with Alice. I bet it was you who was writing all the other comments."

Amy shook her head. "It wasn't, was it?" she said in the same bewildered tone.

Chloe looked at Alice with hatred in her eyes. "Getting your fans to stick up for you?" she sneered, and then she turned back to Mia. "I haven't done anything wrong. When you put yourself out there in the public eye you're setting yourself up for all kinds of comments. We don't all have to hero-worship Alice and Secret. I bet she's only letting *you* help her with her horses to make her look good. She'll dump you like a sack of manure when she's had enough of you."

"Hey, that's not true!" Alice said angrily. But hot-headed Mia shoved Chloe hard, and the older girl fell back. Unfortunately for her she had been standing right next to the muck-heap, and

that's where she landed, sitting right down in the steaming, filthy straw.

"You little—" Red-faced and furious, Chloe leapt to her feet just as a booming voice carried across the yard.

"Alice, Mia, Chloe, come here right now!"

It was June, the district commissioner, and from the look of anger on her face it was clear that she had seen everything. Alice felt a rush of anger. There was no way she or Mia were going to get into trouble after what Chloe had done! She followed Mia and Chloe over to where June was standing, arms folded, with Angus frowning next to her.

"Into the tack room now, all three of you," June said crossly. "And you'd better have a good explanation!"

Chapter 9

"Let me get this straight," June said as she stared at each girl in turn. Alice, Mia and Chloe had just told June their version of events.

"Chloe, you posted a photo online, and made a horrid comment about Alice. Mia, you then took it upon yourself to defend Alice's honour and lost your temper. Is that a fair summary of events?"

Shuffling their feet, Chloe and Mia agreed that it was.

"There have to be some consequences," June then said firmly. "Chloe, remove that photo immediately and apologise to Alice. Mia, you must apologise to Chloe. You'll be on stable duty for the rest of the day, and, Mia, you'll be on tack-cleaning duty. You'll both miss the swimming this afternoon."

"But, June, that's not f—"

Alice was about to say that wasn't fair on Mia. But June wagged her finger.

"Enough!" she said sharply, and Alice fell silent. "Mia, the practice will be good for you. There's a whole heap of tack that needs cleaning for cross country tomorrow. Now come on, I want to hear those apologies right now."

"Sorry Alice." Chloe muttered, not meeting her eyes.

"Sorry Chloe." Mia muttered back, scuffing her feet.

Alice inwardly groaned for Mia, who'd been really excited about the non-riding activity planned for later, a trip to a parent's house in the village with a swimming pool. But she knew the girls had got off lightly. June was known for being tough and it could have been much worse!

"I'll see you later," she said sympathetically to Mia as they left the tack room. Chloe had quickly stalked off.

Mia tried to smile. "It's not so bad I suppose; I *do* need the practice."

Alice was glad Mia was finding the positives in the situation, but she was still furious that because of Chloe, Mia was missing out on the afternoon's fun. Chloe was nothing but trouble.

★

"How was your afternoon?"

It was the end of the day and Alice and Mia were riding back home. Alice, her hair still damp from a fun afternoon at the swimming pool, felt a bit guilty as Mia was hot and dusty after cleaning everyone's tack ready for the cross-country ride in the morning.

"It was OK," Mia replied. "I found a load of stuff in a box. Different polishes and things. I *think* I got it all right. Everything looked super shiny anyway."

"That's good," Alice said, nodding. "I don't mind tack cleaning really."

"You won't tell your mum what happened today, will you?" Mia then asked, her voice small.

Alice smiled and shook her head. "Nope. What happens at camp stays at camp and all that." Then she paused. "And anyway … thank you. I mean, it probably wasn't the best way to go about it, but thanks for sticking up for me."

"That's OK," Mia grinned. Then she looked thoughtful. "What *is* her problem though? She seems so jealous of you."

Alice blew out. "Honestly, I don't know," she said. "She just seems to hate me."

★

"Alice!"

Alice turned to see her friend Amy, phone in hand, looking wildly overexcited. It was the final day of camp, and everyone was looking forward to the cross-country ride. After yesterday's drama, Alice was hoping for a much more relaxed day. She'd totally ignored Chloe, and Chloe had done the same. Although everyone knew what had gone on, they all seemed pretty distracted about the day's cross country ride.

"So, I know something amazing!" Amy put her arm through Alice's as they walked along.

"Has Secret got an invitation to Buckingham

Palace?" Jordan, next to her, joked and Alice rolled her eyes at him.

"No, silly!" Amy laughed. "Better. It turns out your Dupont shoot wasn't such a disaster, after all. Jo couldn't believe it, but one of the few shots they actually took was totally perfect, and they want to use it. She's emailed you and your mum but I bet you haven't even looked at it yet. Look…" She thrust her phone at Alice, who focused on the screen, and she had to admit that the image in front of her was utterly beautiful. It had been edited to look as though she was jumping over a mountain. Secret had never looked better, each muscle clearly defined under his shiny red coat, his mane streaming behind him, and Alice was pleased to note she had a look of fierce determination about her, not some silly grin or her mouth open.

"That's actually pretty cool." She handed the phone back to Amy. "I'm glad they were happy

121

with it. It's certainly better than the photo Chloe put online yesterday!"

Amy frowned. "Yeah. She said it was only a joke but it wasn't a very nice thing to do. But she said sorry, right? Anyway, this Dupont stuff is amazing! In her message Jo says she's going to be in touch with your mum about doing some more stuff. This could be just the start of it, Alice! You're going to be a HUGE star!"

But before Alice could reply she was forced to step aside as Chloe marched through, shooting her a dirty look. There was no doubt she'd overheard Amy.

Amy shook her arm. "Alice!" she demanded. "What do you think? You *have* to say yes when they ring your mum!"

Truthfully Alice didn't know what to think. The Dupont shoot had been pretty stressful in the end. It was amazing to have been sent all the

kit, there was no denying that, but there was too much going on in her head at that moment with Hickstead coming up.

"I'm not so sure it's for me," she replied. "Can I think about it once Hickstead is over?"

Amy rolled her eyes. "I guess," she said. "But please say yes. It's an amazing opportunity. So many people would be so jealous of you right now!"

★

The pony club members were going to be paired off for the cross-country course. But later that morning, as Alice approached the board that had been set up in the yard, she had a bad feeling in the pit of her stomach. She groaned when her instinct was confirmed. Her name was next to Chloe's. Of *all* the people to be paired with. She was hoping she'd be paired with Holly, or Amy, even Hannah. Sighing loudly, she gave Secret a pat, turning him towards his day stable.

"Come on, boy," she said. "You'll have to be on your very best behaviour today."

Chloe clearly wasn't any happier than Alice about their pairing.

"No way!" she said hotly as she approached the board, passing Alice.

"Please can I swap partners?" Alice asked June as she appeared from the kitchen.

"No," June said firmly. "You girls are jumping together at Hickstead in just a few days. I've paired you up deliberately – there's no better way to work as a team than by doing the pairs course. No arguments!"

Chloe huffed as June strode away.

"I don't want to spend any more time with you than I have to!" Alice said, glaring at her. "But we're going to have to get on with it."

Chloe glared right back before stalking off to her

stable, muttering something Alice couldn't hear.

★

The girls warmed up later in complete silence. Not only did Alice have nothing to say to Chloe, but she was having to use all her energy to keep Secret calm. In order to be suitable for everyone the jumps were no more technical than logs or hay bales, but it was the realisation that Alice was going to be cantering across open country and jumping that caused her stomach to flip over. She hacked out regularly over the very same downs, and often popped over little jumps, but she hadn't been on a formal cross-country ride since the awful day her very first pony Honey had suffered a heart attack and died. She was out of her comfort zone and nervous, and she needed to let Chloe know.

"Um…" Alice fell into step with Chloe as she nudged Mac on, walking around as they waited. Each pair was being set off a few minutes apart to give them time to complete the course without running into each other, and Alice and Chloe were last to go. "If you don't mind, could we take it quite steady, just trot in between the jumps?" She was aware that her voice sounded shaky.

Chloe looked at her curiously. "Really?" She raised an eyebrow. "I thought you were the star of pony club with all the gear to match. Don't tell me you're *nervous*?"

Alice sighed. "Well, I am, a bit," she said softly. "It's the first time I've done anything like this on Secret. If we could just take it steady, that would be great."

A strange smile crossed Chloe's face. "Of course," she said. "We'll go as steadily as you like..."

Chapter 10

"Ready, girls?"

The volunteer steward checked his watch. "A couple of minutes to go. Now remember – it's just for fun. Take care and enjoy it!"

Secret seemed to have grown in height as he danced on the spot with every muscle tensed, his red nostrils flared, his eyes firmly fixed on the first jump about a hundred metres from the start.

Mac was much calmer and practically resting a leg as the steward checked his watch again and spoke into his walkie-talkie. Alice might not have wanted to ride with Chloe, but at least her pony was lovely and quiet. That would help steady Secret.

"You'll have your work cut out!" The steward smiled at Alice as Secret half reared, his red mane flying back.

"Yes, hopefully we'll be safe with him," Chloe said.

To Alice's surprise her voice sounded shaky and nervous. Alice frowned, but there was no time to reassure Chloe that Secret wasn't actually going to do anything awful. Raising his hand, the steward started to count backwards from ten.

"Three – two – one, go!"

The steward waved Alice and Chloe on, and, buoyed up, Secret gave the most tremendous leap

into the air.

"Watch it!" Chloe shouted, as Secret cantered sideways into the first jump. Leaping it by miles, Alice clung on tight to a handful of mane as Secret landed and gave a joyful buck. Conscious that the ground was hard, Alice desperately tried to bring him back to her as Secret surged over the turf. Glancing back, she saw the steward grimace; she had to get Secret under control.

They jumped the next, a simple log, and then turned out into the open countryside where a few stewards had parked their cars next to each jump in case of any accidents. Secret had started to settle, much to Alice's relief. She could just see the pair who'd gone ahead of them, Jordan and Holly, cantering up on the hill. Even without being close she could see they were having a brilliant time. Holly had one hand on the reins and they were chatting and laughing as their ponies popped neatly over the low fences. Alice started to relax a little. Even riding next to Chloe, once Secret started to settle, this was actually going to be fun.

But it seemed Mac had other ideas, and to Alice's surprise the grey pony shot past them, causing Secret to veer sideways in alarm.

"Whoa!" cried Alice, feeling the air whip through her ponytail as Mac thundered on. Was Chloe in trouble? The grey pony was going at quite a pace, and Secret, giving a squeal, lengthened his stride, lowering his head in order to keep up.

"Chloe, slow down a bit, or I won't be able to control Secret!"

Had Mac bolted?

"Chloe, are you OK?"

But when Chloe turned her head Alice saw she was smiling. A cool, determined smile. Turning back to the front, Chloe nudged her pony hard and Mac burst forward again as they crossed the

large section of common towards the next fence. There was no one nearby; they had to swing round the corner to the next jump. She was doing it on purpose, Alice realised. She was urging Mac on. And now Alice was losing control.

"Chloe!" she yelled desperately. "This isn't funny! Please slow down!"

She'd make a circle, she decided. Tell a steward what was happening, retire from the course. She had no idea what Chloe was playing at, but this was meant to be a fun activity and it was anything but now.

Sitting deep into the saddle, Alice tried to collect her breathing. "Easy now, boy, easy."

Putting her weight down in her off stirrup, Alice started to make the turn into a circle.

"Oh, help! Help!"

Chloe's desperate screams tore through the air and Alice looked up, not understanding what was happening.

"Please help! Secret bolted and now I can't stop Mac!"

"W-what?" That wasn't true! Chloe had urged *her* pony on past Secret. She'd done it on purpose!

But the scream was real, and as Alice managed to slow Secret she saw Mac had swung sharply round to follow them. But whereas Alice would have gone with the turn, shifting her weight in rhythm with her pony, Chloe had lurched to the side, falling heavily to the hard ground. Alice slowed Secret, swinging him round and going back to help.

June was the steward on the next fence, and was soon running towards Chloe and Mac, but Alice got there first. Leaping off Secret she knelt beside Chloe, who had pulled herself up, holding her hip and wincing. Mac had cantered away, but was now grazing calmly, reins over his head.

"It's OK," Alice said in a voice she hoped was less panicked than she felt. "Are you alright? Where are you hurt?"

And as the girls' eyes met, Alice felt she caught a glimpse of the real Chloe for the first time, who looked unsure and teary. Then June was there.

"Oh goodness, Chloe! What happened?" she said breathlessly. "Can you get up? Or do we need to call for help?"

Gingerly Chloe stretched each limb. "I'm OK," she said, tears now spilling over, and Alice breathed a sigh of relief.

Then Chloe's eyes narrowed. "No thanks to you!" she hissed.

Alice, who'd been in the process of straightening up and dusting the dirt from her jodhpurs gave a start. "What?"

"What do you mean, Chloe?" June asked again. "I couldn't quite see what happened."

Chloe gave a little sob. "Secret bolted, and I couldn't control Mac," she explained as chills started to run up and down Alice's spine.

"And something was wrong with my saddle," Chloe whimpered. "It was fine yesterday, but then it was cleaned. I didn't have any grip. I just couldn't stay on..."

Alice's stomach flipped. Mia had cleaned all the tack yesterday. Was Chloe implying that Mia was behind her fall somehow?

"That's not true!" Alice blurted out. "You just fell. You lost your balance. I saw!"

Chloe flashed her an angry look. "I didn't!" she hissed. "My saddle was extra slippery. There was no way I could stay on!"

"I'll need to check the saddle and talk to Mia..." June said gravely.

Alice felt fury rising in her stomach. "That's rubbish!" she said before she could stop herself.

134

"You're lying! You're lying about the saddle and you're lying about Secret bolting. What is *wrong* with you?"

"Hold it right there, girls," June said sternly, before lifting her walkie-talkie. "Chloe Williams has had a fall, so we'll need to get her back to base," she said into the receiver, pausing for a moment until she received a response from the other person. She turned back to them. "A car is coming down for you Chloe. Alice, you can come back with me. Let me go and get Mac."

As June headed off to catch the sweet grey pony Alice threw Chloe a furious look. "What are you playing at?" she hissed. "Why did you say that Secret caused Mac to bolt?"

Chloe smiled. "Well," she said, *"everyone* saw Secret going crazy at the start, didn't they?"

"But you lied!" Alice continued. "And Mia had nothing to do with you falling. That's not fair!"

Chloe glared back. "Didn't she? How do you know? She has no idea how to clean tack!" she spat. "She doesn't know a thing about horses. What makes her so special?"

Alice couldn't even begin to understand what Chloe meant by that, but their argument was interrupted by June's shouts. Looking up, Alice saw immediately what the problem was. Mac had stood on his reins, much like Secret had when Mia had held him after the jumping lesson, but Mac's reins had snapped, and he was now cantering away in a panic. And as his broken reins and one flapping stirrup flew around him it seemed to upset him further until the canter turned into a blind gallop.

June was shouting into her walkie-talkie. "Loose pony! Is the gate open for the car?"

Something indecipherable came back over the walkie-talkie and June put a hand on her forehead,

her face showing the seriousness of the situation. "We need to stop him; he'll get straight on to the road!"

"Mac!" Chloe said in a trembling voice, clutching her hip as she tried to get to her feet. "Somebody please help him!"

June set off towards her car, parked up next to the cross country fence, but Alice knew that it would take her some time to reach the downs. For a second Alice felt her back prickle with sweat as she had a flashback to when Lachlan, her mum's old pony, had been hit by a car and killed on a stretch of road near here. She couldn't let that happen again. Chloe might be awful, but it wasn't her pony's fault. The fastest way to catch a loose pony was by pony, and Alice had a fast pony who was dancing about next to her, plunging forward, as if telling Alice that they needed to go, and now.

Vaulting on, Alice gathered up her reins. "I'll get

him," she said to Chloe, who was white with fear. "Secret will catch him up."

And wheeling round she only had to nudge Secret and he bounded forward, his long red legs eating up the ground as Alice flattened herself against his neck, the warm air whipping her face, the thud of Secret's hooves on the hard ground matching the thud of her heart.

She could see the grey pony up ahead. He was slowing slightly, but heading straight towards the open gate. Neither June nor one of the helpers from camp had reached the road yet. With one final burst of speed Alice drew level with Mac, whose sides were foamy with sweat as the broken reins came perilously close to tripping him. She thought of Finn, how he could throw himself over the side of a pony so that he was almost brushing the floor, and, taking a deep breath, Alice pushed all her weight into one stirrup and

leaned right over, grabbing Mac's trailing reins and pulling hard.

"I'm sorry, boy!" she cried to Mac, knowing she was going to yank him in the mouth, but it was better than getting hit by a car. For a few precarious seconds Mac didn't slow down and Alice was having to cling on to Secret with all the strength she had in her other hand. Thankfully Secret remained in perfect step with Mac, and gradually the grey pony slowed to a canter, then a trot, before coming to a halt, his sides heaving. Alice thought again of Finn and the crazy stunts he performed on horseback, and fought the urge to laugh out loud, the adrenalin of the chase coursing through her blood.

At that moment a car pulled up next to the open gate, blocking it. Had Alice not caught Mac, he would have been on the road. Once again, she shuddered, the image of Lachlan clear in her mind, and she batted the thought away. Mac was safe. Secret was safe. A moment later another car arrived, with Chloe in the passenger seat.

June jumped out of the car. "Well done," she said to Alice. "That was some good riding." Then she paused. "I need to get Chloe back to Hilltops and sort her out."

"Chloe isn't telling the truth," Alice said breathlessly. "She's always had it in for me and now she hates Mia too."

June nodded thoughtfully. "It's clear something is going on, but I don't think the middle of a field is the right place to sort it out," she said firmly. "Are you happy to walk Mac back? I don't think Chloe will be able to ride."

Alice nodded and then June hopped back in her car. Secret nuzzled Mac affectionately as Alice clucked her pony forward. Mac was a sweet pony, so he followed happily behind. He seemed fine,

if a little tired. Alice took it slowly, aware they'd just had a very fast gallop. It took about twenty minutes to get back to Hilltops. As Alice and Chloe had been the last pair to go around the cross-country course, everyone was already back in the yard tending to their ponies. As she walked towards the stables she was aware that everyone was staring at her and whispering to each other.

Amy came forward to help her with the two ponies. She looked worried.

"What's going on?" asked Alice.

Amy looked at Alice. "It's Mia," she said in a low voice. "June got back and called Mia straight into her office. Something about a saddle?"

Alice felt her blood run cold. "Where is she now?"

Amy shook her head. "She's headed off somewhere on Porridge. Someone tried to call her mum but there was no answer."

"Her mum works shifts," Alice said. "Oh, I hope she's OK! You know she didn't have anything to do with this right?" she said and Amy pulled a face.

"I believe you!" she said. "It's all crazy. Nobody knows what's going on!"

Alice hated the thought of Mia heading off alone. Where could she be? But then Alice thought about where Mia was happiest, and she knew that Park Farm was the first place she should check.

Chapter 11

Alice arrived home to the sound of desperate sobbing coming from Porridge's stable. She'd left the stables pretty much right away, without waiting to speak to June. She just had to hope she wasn't going to get into trouble. To her relief, as she looked over the stable door Porridge gave a whinny, peering out from under his thick black forelock.

Tying Secret up, Alice went into the Shetland's stable. Mia was curled up at the back in the straw, hands over her face as she cried.

"Mia?" Alice said gently, and the younger girl looked up, her eyes red.

She flinched. "I didn't do anything wrong!" she hiccupped, sounding both devastated and defiant.

"I know," Alice said, nodding. "I know you didn't. For some reason Chloe has it in for me, and now you. I don't know what she's playing at, but I believe you!"

Mia sniffed. "She said something really weird yesterday, when it was just me and her left on the yard and I was cleaning tack," she said in a trembling voice. "She said you and your mum would tell me to go eventually, that I wouldn't be good enough for you." She held her chin up. "I told her to stick it obviously, but, Alice, what did she mean?"

Alice shook her head. "Why would we tell you to go? I mean, why would she think that...? Oh!"

Like a bolt of lightning had hit the stable, she suddenly knew where she'd seen Chloe before. It wasn't at a show; it wasn't from school. Chloe Williams had been here, on the yard.

★

Feed invoices, vet bills ... passports. Alice frowned as she flicked through the folders in the filing cabinet. Her mum kept *everything* relating to her business, so there had to be something that would prove Chloe had visited the yard. Alice knew it had been about the time she'd been backing Secret, before the summer when she'd first met Finn. She'd been struggling hugely with Secret. Her mum had been run off her feet trying to find someone else to ride the ponies at shows alongside Alice and had advertised in the local saddlery shop. Of course shortly after Finn had come along

★
★
145 ★

and ridden Archie, one of Josephine's clients' best ponies, and there had been no need to find anyone else. But before that someone had answered the ad. Alice could remember now. It was coming back to her like watching an old movie, watching the stills frame by frame.

She'd been in the yard and Chloe had come up. Alice had been crying, she recalled with a hot flood of shame. It had been the day Secret had totally refused to trot at a show, then he'd got home and promptly jumped out of his field. Alice had been at her lowest point, aware Secret was too much for her, and when a car had pulled up she'd hidden in the stables, embarrassed by her tear-stained face. She'd caught a glimpse of a girl around her own age. When she'd asked her mum later that evening about the visitor to the yard, her mum had shaken her head.

"Not right," her mum had said dismissively.

"Back to the drawing board."

And that had been that.

"There it is!" Alice had found what she'd been looking for. The original advert, a neat and punctual paragraph in type, and a scrawl next to it in biro in her mum's handwriting.

Chloe W. – 3 p.m. 27 April trial.

And again, Alice was taken back to that moment, running to hide in a stable as the girl and her mum got out of the car. They'd walked past just as Alice had bolted the door and pressed her face into Secret's neck, and Alice could see the girl's eyes, the clearest of blues, her expression quizzical. She'd smiled at her, and Alice hadn't smiled back. And worse, the girl had tried talking to her; she'd complimented Secret. Alice hadn't been able to respond, hadn't been able to do anything but turn away, unable to talk for fear of crying. It had been an awful day, and she had no idea who the girl was or why she was there. But she knew now. She'd worked it out. Chloe had come to try out for a riding job, and her mum had turned her down. And Chloe seemed to blame Alice for that.

★

"So what do we do?" Mia sniffed as Alice relayed the information to her. "It doesn't prove anything."

Alice frowned. "I know. But I'm guessing Chloe holds a grudge. I *know* Secret didn't wind up Mac this morning."

"And I didn't do anything to her saddle!" Mia said. "I wouldn't even know how to. *And* one of the grooms came in and said I'd done a good job. Maybe she can back me up?"

"So we'll go and explain everything to June," Alice said more confidently than she felt. She knew the steward who had waved her and Chloe off at the start of the cross country would back up Chloe's claims about Secret, and Mia *had* been left

alone to clean tack. She bit her lip. "All we can do is tell the truth."

Mia nodded, and Alice felt her resolve strengthen. All Mia had wanted was a chance to ride ponies. It hadn't been her fault she'd been dragged into this mess between Chloe and Alice, a mess Alice hadn't even realised existed until the last hour!

A beep from her pocket broke the mood and pulling her phone out, Alice stared at the message from Amy.

Where are you?!?! Come back! It's all going off here. Hannah's dad came to see us. The controls for the arena sprinkler were set off deliberately ... by Chloe!!!

★

"We need to head back."

Amy's text message had changed everything. Alice now had proof that Chloe had been trying to get at Alice!

"How will we get there?" Mia said in a small voice. "The ponies are tired and your mum and dad are out."

Alice thought for a moment, then grinned. "Let's use the quad bike. Fergus lets me ride around the fields now. Here, I'll find you a helmet. Let's go!"

And with Mia clinging to Alice's waist, Alice turned the key in the ignition and took a deep breath, heading out towards the fields and the path over the downs towards Hilltops.

"Woooo!" she heard Mia cry behind her. "This is awesome!"

Alice smiled, despite the seriousness of the situation. But up ahead she saw a figure running towards them. A familiar figure with long dark hair and bright blue eyes, crying desperately. Alice swallowed hard, slowing the bike and turning the ignition key off. Chloe.

★

Chloe had been so upset at first that Alice could barely understand her. Leaving the quad bike at the top of the farm, she and Mia walked Chloe back down into the yard, and Alice ran into the house for a glass of water. Carrying it back out to the stables, she led Chloe into the cool of the barn. Handing the glass to her, she sat down next to her until Chloe had blown her nose and wiped her eyes. Alice hated seeing anyone upset, but Chloe's attempt to frame Mia and Alice over the disastrous cross-country ride *and* her messages *and* the sabotage of the sprinklers couldn't easily be forgiven.

"What's going on?" Alice asked Chloe.

Chloe sniffed, plucking the sleeve of her shirt. "It went too far," she said, her voice upset yet oddly defiant. "*I* went too far."

"Go on," Alice said quietly as Mia chewed on her thumbnail, listening intently as she perched on a shavings bale.

"I hated you. I mean, I *really* hated you!" Chloe lifted her tear-stained face to look right at Alice. "All I wanted was to ride ponies, just like you, and you didn't even remember me! You just ignored me when I came here, and your mum couldn't care less that she'd crushed my dream. She decided I didn't fit in here, and so she wouldn't even give me a chance."

Alice shook her head. "It wasn't like that! I remember now that you came here to ride, to try out. But I honestly didn't mean to ignore you," she said. "I'd had a really bad day. Secret had been a nightmare and Mum was angry at me! I was so upset and ashamed I didn't want to see anyone. I felt like such a failure."

Chloe paused for a moment. "But you could get up the next day and ride again," she said quietly. "I couldn't."

"What do you mean?" Alice asked, feeling confused. "We're not the only yard around."

"You don't understand!" Chloe said, her eyes suddenly flashing with fury. "That was my chance! After that, my parents said I should concentrate on other stuff. I ended up having to get a Saturday job washing up in a café. I didn't ride for almost two years!"

Feeling the full force of Chloe's anger, Alice started to understand why the other girl hated her so much. She tried to imagine not being able to ride for two years. She'd given up, when Honey had died, but that had been her choice. It hadn't been taken away from her.

"But then, my dad got a new job," Chloe continued. "We had enough money for lessons, and even Mac! He was my dream come true. But then I met you at pony club, and you *still* didn't remember me," she glared at Alice. "It wasn't easy for me. And then you, with all your success, everyone looking up to you like you were some sort of hero. It was all so easy for you!"

Alice looked at Chloe in amazement.

"But that's not how it is at all!" she cried angrily. "If you'd seen those early days with Secret, you'd know how hard it was. And I know I'm lucky to live with ponies, I know that. But the yard, it's my mum's life, it's her business. I know she wouldn't have meant to have upset you!"

"But what do you have that makes you so special," Chloe sniffed, looking at Mia now. "Why did *you* get the chance?"

Alice now understood all the resentment, the snide remarks. Chloe had never forgotten how she'd been made to feel. And then Mia, a total novice, had been allowed into the yard, even given the ride on one of her mum's very best ponies. She could see how that looked to Chloe.

And how much it still hurt her.

"I think I understand how you felt," Alice said. "But blaming me for Mac bolting and blaming Mia for your fall?" she shook her head. "That was downright nasty."

"I know," Chloe whispered, shamefaced. "I just snapped. I was going to sort of jump off and make it look like I'd fallen, no one would have seen me on that bit of the course and it would have been your word against mine … but it went wrong and I really did fall."

Alice frowned.

"Why did you say your tack had been tampered with?"

"It was a split-second thing," Chloe plucked harder at her sleeve. "I wasn't thinking. I was embarrassed I fell when I should have been able to stay on. I thought perhaps if I said my saddle was slippery, I could somehow blame Mia and make out she used the wrong polish on it or something…" Her voice trailed away.

"Wow." Was all Alice could manage.

Seeing her horrified face, Chloe nodded. "I know it was crazy. All I wanted was for you to feel as bad as I did! When I heard you got your deal with that posh riding clothes company, I just saw red. But then Mac…" She started to cry again. "Mac could have been injured, killed even on the road, and you saved him. I can never thank you enough."

"I couldn't let anything happen to him," Alice said quietly.

"I know, and I owe you everything," Chloe wiped her eyes on her sleeve. "And now I can see I went way too far. It should have been enough for me … seeing you getting squirted by the water, I wanted you to feel embarrassed. But then when Mia shoved me I was so angry. And you *still* had

no idea who I was!"

"I can't believe you set the arena sprinklers off," Alice said slowly.

Chloe gave a short, bitter laugh. "I found the controls in the tack room and looked it up online. I just wanted to embarrass you, everyone was crowding around you at that photo shoot like you were the queen or something!" She said. Then her face dropped. "But Hannah's dad was looking back at the CCTV to see if I could prove Mia cleaned my saddle, and found the bit of me going in the day before."

Alice was silent for a few moments while it all sank in. Despite everything, she actually felt sorry for Chloe. She was so hell bent on getting revenge that things had got totally out of control.

An anxious knock on the door interrupted the conversation and Alice's mum came in.

"Girls," she said in a relieved voice. "I've had a

call from June. I went straight to Hilltops, we must have passed each other on different routes." Then turning to Chloe, she smiled kindly. "It's Chloe Williams, isn't it? I've just been talking to your dad."

Alice's mum listened quietly as Chloe recounted the whole story, from her trial ride at the yard to Josephine's phone call telling her she wasn't going to get the job, to meeting Alice at pony club.

"All you told my dad was that I wasn't right," Chloe said. "That was it!"

Alice's mum nodded and Alice could see she realised the effect that the rejection phone call had made.

"Chloe, I'm sorry, I really am, that I made you feel like you weren't good enough to work here," she said gently. "I hadn't realised how much it meant to you. You see, I have lots of ponies on this yard who don't belong to me, and I needed

an experienced rider to help me at shows." She paused. "I could see you loved horses, very much, and had it not been my business then of course you could have ridden for me. But I had a business to run. I needed a rider whom I didn't have to teach." She glanced at Mia. "But things change, life changes. Had it been a year or two on, then it would have been different." She stood up, dusting off her shorts. "You have a lovely pony now Chloe," she said. "Just enjoy him, enjoy what you have right now, try not to hold on to the past."

Chloe sniffed, and nodded as Josephine briefly placed a hand on her arm before heading back out.

"Thank you," she said quietly.

"How is Mac?" Alice asked gently. Chloe obviously adored her grey pony, she'd called him her *dream come true*. Chloe looked at the floor.

"He's slightly footsore," she said in a trembling voice. "So he couldn't jump at Hickstead now. Not that I'd be able to, I'll be getting kicked out of the branch, for sure."

So they were down to just three team members now, Alice realised, imagining Jordan and Amy's disappointment. But she couldn't think about it right at that moment.

"I'm sorry," she said. And she really meant it.

"Hey," Chloe gave a small smile. "It's my fault. He'll be OK with a few days rest. And," she paused. "Your mum's right. I just need to enjoy him."

The sound of a car broke the silence that followed, and peering out from behind the door, Alice recognised the dusty 4x4 that belonged to June. Angus was in the passenger seat.

Chloe straightened her pony tail, and stood up, taking a deep breath.

"Guess I'd better go and face the music," she said, turning to Alice. "Thank you for catching Mac. And I'm sorry, I really am. For everything."

Chapter 12

"Well," Amy said, grinning, "we've had some camp dramas over the years, but that was something else!" She bit into her burger. "What a nightmare Chloe turned out to be. I can't believe it!"

It was later that afternoon and the pony clubbers were at the barbecue. Alice and Mia had come back to join their friends.

Alice frowned, taking a bite of her own burger. "I don't think Chloe was a total nightmare," she said, and Amy looked at her in surprise. "I think she just got completely carried away. She thought I was someone I wasn't and wanted to make me feel as bad as she once had."

She thought of Chloe, quiet and tear-stained as her dad picked her and Mac up earlier. The sweet grey pony would be fine after a few days' rest. Alice hadn't exactly hugged Chloe goodbye, but she had wished her luck, and she genuinely hoped Chloe would be OK.

"You're nicer than I'd have been," Amy said, and then her expression changed as her shoulders slumped. "I'm still gutted, though. To think we should all be getting ready for Hickstead now."

"I know," Alice said sadly as the two girls headed back to the barbecue for a second burger. "I guess Angus can't find anyone to take the fourth place?"

Amy shook her head. "Nope. Lola will be in Portugal and Sam's going to Florida with his grandparents. And Hannah, who *would* have been able to, is off to the dressage nationals."

Their conversation was interrupted by Angus. "Alice, can I have a word?"

Puzzled, Alice followed their showjumping instructor to a quieter section of the yard, still clutching her burger.

"You've probably heard from Amy that I've had no luck replacing Chloe on the team." He ran a hand through his jet-black hair, reminding Alice briefly of Finn.

"I know," Alice said sadly.

"No pony is up to standard, and even if we found a pony, we don't have a rider." Angus sighed. "But all's not totally lost," he continued with a brief smile. "I can still enter you an individual ... if you'd like? As our strongest pairing, it makes sense. Secret has the best chance and we can still put Hilltops on the map."

"Wow, um, really?" Alice hadn't expected this. But she was used to jumping alone and she knew Angus was desperate to raise the credibility of their tiny branch.

"Will you do it?" Angus said hopefully. "I've had a quick word with Amy and Jordan and they both agreed you'd be the best choice. And, Alice, I think if you do well … this could be your time to shine. People are starting to take notice of you."

Alice thought about it for a moment. "OK," she said, nodding. "I'll do it. But I'm not doing it for me – I'm doing it for Hilltops."

"Super," Angus smiled. "That's still something, isn't it?"

But Alice didn't feel the usual buzz of excitement. She'd do her best, she always would, but the last few months of training had been brilliant, and she

wished they could show off as a branch, as a team, as friends.

★

"Alice!"

Her mum's voice carried up the stairs where Alice was lying on her bed reading *Horse & Hound*. "Phone for you."

Running down, Alice looked at her mum who had her hand over the speaker and a smile on her face. "It's Devon Jenkins," she mouthed, and Alice gaped at her.

Devon Jenkins, who Alice had met at Olympia, was her hero! They had kept in contact, and Alice was waiting for a gap in Devon's schedule to go there for work experience.

"H-hello?" she said, wishing she didn't sound so young on the phone.

"Alice!" Devon said happily. "How are you? I just wanted to let you know I haven't forgotten about you and as soon as Hickstead is over I'm going to sit down in my office and look at the diary," she said, and Alice gave a start of excitement. She was so looking forward to taking Secret to Devon's yard!

"But what about meeting up at Hickstead?" Devon then said. "I know you're jumping with your pony club team, right? Want a hand in the warm-up?"

Alice sighed, imagining how excited Jordan and Amy would have been to have the chance to jump in front of Devon.

"It's just me now," she explained sadly.

"Oh!" Devon said. "But that's still a good thing, isn't it?"

"Yes." Alice tried to explain. "It just that we were so excited about going as a team. But there's been a bit of drama over the last week or so…" And before she could stop herself, she was telling

Devon everything that had happened, and that the team were now a rider and a pony short.

"Hmmm," Devon said thoughtfully. "I have an amazing pony in at the moment who'd suit the class, but she's pretty hot-headed. I'd be happy for you to ride her. But I guess that still leaves you a team member down?"

Alice blinked. She hadn't expected Devon to start suggesting solutions!

"That's really kind, Devon, but—" Alice started to say. And then, like the sun breaking, a plan started to form in her mind.

"Well, the offer is there," Devon said. "I'd ride her myself if I wasn't miles too old." She chuckled. "Think about it anyway."

Alice knew she was going to think of nothing else. This could be Hilltops' last chance to ride as a team at Hickstead!

★

It was hard to sleep. The heat from the day seemed to close in with the dark, the air lying like a heavy cloak round Alice as she tossed and turned in bed, listening to the dawn chorus that had started around three a.m. She, her mum and Mia were leaving for Hickstead later that morning, ready for Mia's show class the following day, and then staying on another night for Alice's individual the day after. Jordan and Amy were coming to watch, and Alice knew they were putting on brave faces about not jumping themselves.

All night Alice had been thinking about Devon's offer. The idea she'd had was taking shape, but she wasn't sure if it was completely ridiculous, and too risky to boot. It was no good; she had to get up. Checking her watch, she worked out that it was a couple of hours later in Spain, and decided to call her best friend, Finn. He'd be up; he always was, riding out before breakfast because it was

even hotter over there. Slipping on her flip-flops, she padded downstairs in her short pyjamas and headed out into the yard where streaks of pink were dancing across the sky, the ponies grazing out in the fields. Secret gave a shrill whinny and Alice smiled, putting her fingers to her lips.

"Shhh," she said, climbing through the post and rail and placing her arms round his strong red neck. "Don't you go waking everyone up."

Then, sitting down on the dusty ground only slightly dampened by the dew, she found Finn on her phone, a photo of him and Horatio next to his name.

"Hey!" His voice, so familiar, so warm, greeted her on the second ring. "Isn't it, like, four in the morning with you?"

"Five," Alice smiled. "But I wanted to talk to you."

A whinny, probably Horatio's, rang out, and

pressing the phone to her ear Alice could just make out the clip-clop of hooves on hard earth.

"Go on," Finn said. "I'm riding. It will be like I'm back in England almost, chatting to you. Apart from the fact it's hotter than the sun out here, and I'm looking at orange trees instead of hedges."

Alice, who'd been sent plenty of photos of where Finn was staying, closed her eyes, imagining the sweet smell of oranges warmed by the heat of the sun. She took a deep breath, suddenly missing her friend desperately and their long, long chats while they hacked out. "Would you think I was crazy, if I told you I was considering giving up my place in the individual on Secret, so that we could still have a team? I mean … letting someone else ride him? Someone I really trusted?"

There was a pause.

"No," Finn said in a measured tone. "I know you'd only do that if you thought you were doing

the right thing. I know how much Hickstead means to you. Is that someone Mia?"

Alice had messaged Finn, keeping him up to date, so he knew everything.

"Yes," she said. "Mia."

She'd had the thought in her head, ever since Devon's call. Devon could lend a pony to the team – to Alice – but they were still a rider short. And there was one rider who hadn't been considered. Someone who was fearless, who was a complete natural, someone who'd got to know Secret over the past few weeks. Mia.

"Devon's offered me a pony," Alice went on. "But only I can ride her and so I would need to trust Secret with Mia. And I do."

Alice had rung Devon back before she talked to the rest of the team, to make absolutely sure Devon was happy to lend her the pony. Devon had been thrilled, and she and Alice had talked at length about the mare in question.

"Whoa," Finn said. "I mean, that's amazing, but it's pretty short notice, isn't it?"

"Yep." Alice chewed on her thumbnail. "But we're all up at Hickstead anyway and I know Amy and Jordan would jump at the chance to come and, if it works, it might just be the answer."

"And your individual?" Finn questioned.

"I'd have to give it up." Alice took a deep breath, feeling a twinge of regret. If everyone agreed and surely they would, she was giving up the chance to see Hickstead from between Secret's red ears. But there was always next year, and possibly the year after that, too. She knew how much the team competition meant to Hilltops. How hard they'd worked.

Chapter 13

"Me?"

Mia looked shocked as Alice sat down with her later that morning. Mia had arrived after breakfast, bags packed, ready to go away to the biggest show of her life.

"You want *me* to ride Secret?" Mia repeated and Alice nodded, a bubble of anxiety starting to surface. Was this too much to ask?

"Yes," Alice said. "If you want to."

Alice's mum smiled. "I think you'd be fine with him," she said. "When Alice told me about her plan I did hesitate. But –" she looked at her daughter – "Alice knows Secret so well. Believe me, she wouldn't let just anyone ride him."

Alice smiled back at her mum, who gave her hand a quick squeeze. She had gone back into the house after her conversation with Finn and waited for her mum to get up before telling her.

Her mum had hugged her. "I trust you," she'd said, and that had meant everything to Alice.

Mia looked thoughtful. "But you'd be giving up your place in the individual competition," she said quietly, and Alice nodded again, taking a deep breath.

"Yes," she said. "But I've got another pony to ride in the team. And this is about Hilltops, not me. I'll explain everything in the lorry on the way."

There was a pause, before a grin spread slowly across Mia's face. "I think I might be dreaming," she said happily. "Yes. I'll do it; I'll ride Secret. Bring it on!"

★

Alice had hugged Secret extra tight after he'd bounded up the ramp of the lorry in his usual enthusiastic way. "It's not going to be like normal, boy," she'd whispered in his ear as she tied him up next to Porridge. "But I know I can trust you."

On the journey to the show Alice thought back to when she had told people about her idea earlier that day. Angus had been over the moon. Alice knew he would have been a hundred per cent supportive of her in the individual competition, but he'd put so much energy and work into the team – everyone knew how disappointed he'd been when it had fallen apart.

Amy had been quite tearful when Alice had

headed over to Hilltops to tell her the news. "Are we really all going together? We're still jumping?" she'd cried, throwing her arms round Alice, as Jordan whooped with delight and punched the air.

Alice had nodded, hugging Amy back. "Yes, we're still going. Hilltops is going to Hickstead!"

Amy wiped her eyes. "And you're really letting Mia ride Secret?"

"Yes again," Alice said, pushing aside the little twang of regret she felt. "It's the best way. Mia's got to know Secret, and Devon thinks I'll be fine with her pony. It's a risk, but I think it'll work."

"When will Mia get a chance to practise with Secret, though?" Amy had asked. "She's only ridden him once before, hasn't she?"

"The day we get there and after her class on Porridge," Alice had replied more confidently than she'd felt. "But she handles him every day and he really likes her. I've just got to trust Secret.

176

He knows what to do."

"Wow." Amy had smiled, before throwing her arms round Alice again and quickstepping around with her in a sort of crazy dance. "We're going to Hickstead!" she'd grinned, and Alice knew then she'd made the right choice. She just hoped it would work!

Mia, next to Alice in the lorry, brought her back into the present as she turned to Alice excitedly, nudging her arm. "Look," she said, pointing out the yellow signs. "We're nearly there."

Alice's mum smiled, easing the lorry down a gear as she prepared to come off the slip road. It was a journey Alice had done many, many times in the past, but never like this. This time she was part of a team!

★

Porridge and Secret soon settled into their temporary stables. Alice and Mia had lugged their equipment back and forth from the lorry, bumping tack trunks over the dry and dusty ground, a stark contrast to the emerald green of the beautiful arenas, which had been well watered in preparation for the big show.

Alice had texted Devon to let her know she'd arrived. She could still hardly believe she was friends with the showjumper, who was idolised by pony clubbers up and down the country. In her early twenties, famous for her fearless jumping style, Devon was hugely successful. She'd worked so hard to get to the top after a terrible start with a dodgy sponsor, and Alice knew that underneath her friendly, bubbly exterior, she was driven and pin-sharp.

Perfect, the reply read. *When I've finished my class I'll come and find you. Violetta is in Block 2b, Stable 4. Dark brown mare.*

Curious, Alice wandered over to the block,

recognising the tack trunk Devon had had at Olympia with her initials on the side. One stable was empty, probably belonging to the horse Devon was currently jumping. The other was occupied by a dark brown mare with rich dapples running through her coat, her mane and tail a beautiful burnished copper. She was exquisite, Alice thought, breathing in. Not Secret, but lovely all the same.

"Hi, girl," she said, extending her hand. "It's good to meet you."

The mare eyed her warily, stretching her neck forward. Alice let the pony sniff her hand for a few seconds before the mare put her ears back, and turned back to eating her hay. Devon had told Alice that Violetta could be quite aloof, and didn't enjoy loads of fuss. She was certainly not like Secret. Even if you were a stranger, Secret would be all over you: investigating pockets, nudging your arms, brushing his soft, bristly whiskers through your hair. For Alice, who loved to hug every pony she met, it was a bit deflating. She hoped she and Violetta could become friends!

"Alice!"

It was Devon, leading a lovely grey horse. A green rosette was clipped to the bridle and Devon was smiling from ear to ear as she gave Alice a big hug. "How are you?" she asked, placing a head collar over the grey's bridle.

"Good," Alice smiled. "How did you do?" She gestured at the rosette.

"Ah, he was a very clever boy." Devon gave the big horse a kiss on his pink nose. "This is Danny; he's one of my up-and-coming stars." She straightened up. "So, did you meet Violetta? What do you think?"

"She's beautiful," Alice said truthfully. "Thank you."

"She sure is," Devon said, nodding. "But she is sharp. She's talented but not as forgiving as Secret is. But I've seen you ride. She's similar to him; you need to sit quietly and let her jump. She settles about halfway round. Even if you think she won't."

Alice nodded, feeling a bit sick. She knew Secret like the back of her hand. She knew how every jump would feel for Mia, how he would feel like he was bouncing on the spot as they passed through the start, how his stride would lengthen and he would take off perfectly for each fence. She knew how he would ping through the doubles like a rubber ball, how he could turn his body, minnow-like, in mid-air ready for the next jump, shaving off those precious seconds so his time would be completely unbeatable. She swallowed hard. Back at Hilltops, with Amy and Jordan and Mia over the moon at being part of the team, this had seemed a brilliant plan. But now, with only a couple of opportunities to ride Violetta and at the thought of looking through those brown ears instead of the familiar, cheerful red ones, it suddenly felt like the worst idea in the world.

As if sensing her nerves, Devon smiled and squeezed her hand. "Hey," she said gently. "It'll be OK. You're a good enough rider for Violetta. I wouldn't let you jump her otherwise. And you've made Secret the pony he is; that's your hard work. He'll look after Mia. I believe in you both."

★

Alice tried to hold on to Devon's words but she knew she had to put aside her own fears while Mia had her first warm-up session on Secret. Porridge, who hardly needed any preparation, had already had a short hack around the famous grounds and was as relaxed and as happy as ever back in his stable munching on hay. But Secret burst out of his

stable like a racehorse and Alice noticed a look of panic cross Mia's face. She had to look confident, so Mia would feel the same.

"OK," she said, and Mia gave a nervous smile. "It's hard to explain, but Secret has never actually done anything truly scary. It's like…" She tried to think of the right analogy. "It's like riding the crest of a wave, one that never actually breaks."

Mia looked at her in amazement before bursting into fits of giggles. "That's deep!" She chuckled and Alice smiled slightly bashfully. "But I get it," Mia continued. "I totally get what you're saying."

The laughter seemed to relax her and soon she was in the saddle after a leg up from Alice. Secret was small, no bigger than thirteen hands. Alice knew she was getting taller every day, but Mia, who was petite, looked perfect on him.

Gathering up her reins, Mia looked down left and right and then grinned. "I'm actually riding Redgrove Secret at *Hickstead*," she said. "Amazing!"

Secret looked at Alice, his eyes soft, his ears pricked forward, just like on the downs when Mia had ridden him home. Mia was familiar to Secret, a friend of Alice's and therefore a friend of his. Plus, Mia had won Secret over with pockets stuffed full of pony nuts and a kiss for him and every pony in the yard each morning!

Look after her, boy, Alice thought, hoping he could hear her somehow and sense how important this was. Then she gave Mia a thumbs up. "Ready?"

★

Alice called Mia into the centre of the warm-up after watching her walk, trot and canter on both reins. Secret had looked surprisingly calm, which was the first hurdle overcome. So far he'd ignored most of the comings and goings.

"Shall I put up a cross pole?"

★
★   ★
184

Alice's mum, who was watching with her, gestured towards the warm-up jumps, and Alice nodded. "Yep," she said. "Thanks, Mum. Start low for now."

Mia halted Secret next to her, and Alice gave him a pat as he nudged her arm. He seemed to be looking for approval, and it brought a lump to Alice's throat.

"So…" She looked up at the younger girl, who was listening intently, waiting for instructions. "He's going to get excited now. He'll focus on that jump, and you'll feel like he's going out of control. You need to sit quietly, give him his head with your reins, sit deep into your saddle, and just breathe." She half smiled, thinking of this being said to her almost two years ago by Angus as she attended her first disastrous lessons. And now here she was, repeating them almost word to word to someone else.

Mia nodded. "Got it. I watched you do that at Hilltops, when you were training."

"Sure you're OK?" Alice said, looking right at her friend. "You honestly don't have to do this if you don't want to."

Mia smiled. "I'm honestly sure. Surer than I've ever been!"

As Alice went back to join her mum at the side of the ring, Mia nudged Secret on lightly, pushing him into his trademark floating trot, asking him to move into canter and completing a circle before rounding the corner. It was weird, Alice thought, watching Secret's expression change. She knew what it felt like, but now she could see what it looked like. It was as though he sharpened into focus. She could almost see the energy buzzing around him as he lengthened his stride, his eyes firmly focused on the red-and-white-coloured poles. He looked powerful,

formidable. He looked incredible.

"Oh, good girl," her mum muttered. "Look how quietly she's sitting, Alice."

"Am I doing the right thing, Mum?" Alice asked anxiously.

Her mum smiled. "Yes," she said. "I know you would have had the best chance in the individual with Secret. But sometimes it's about the bigger picture, isn't it?" She patted Alice's arm. "I'm really proud of you."

Mia was at one with Secret, her hands feather-light, a look of determination on her face as Secret's canter powered into the jump. Alice felt her own body rise as he jumped the poles, as if she was jumping it with him. Secret landed in a burst of power, and just as Alice had told her to Mia sat quietly, not pulling him back, but letting him surge on. Rounding the corner, she slowed to a trot.

"That," Mia called over, her whole face lit up with a grin, "was amazing!"

And Alice let out a breath, one that she hadn't even realised she'd been holding.

★

Devon had been right about her mare being sharp. Violetta was taller than Secret but slender and fine-legged. The dark brown mare danced down to the warm-up arena like a leaf being blown along in a breeze, curling her whole body sideways as she looked at everything, from the bins and other horses to dogs on leads and signposts.

"She's a bit spooky!" Devon, walking besides them, remarked cheerfully. "Pain to hack out."

Alice tried to smile, hoping it would help relax her whole body. She knew it was silly, but she was glad Secret couldn't see her right now, even though she knew he would on the day of the competition. She didn't want him to get upset! As she entered

the warm-up arena Violetta danced from side to side, eager to keep moving.

Devon perched on the fence to watch. "Remember, just like Secret, you think she might boil over."

Violetta's trot and canter were much choppier than Secret's, and Alice took a few laps of the arena to get used to her paces, which were so different to Secret's rocking horse strides. Encouraged by Devon, they jumped over a few cross poles, before Devon put up a simple spread. Violetta charged into it, and Alice had a moment of panic, causing Violetta to take off slightly early, catching the back rail with her hoof.

"Don't worry!" Devon called, putting the green-and-white pole back up. "Try again – softer with your hands this time."

And so Alice and Violetta jumped a few more times before Alice slowed to a walk, giving

189

Violetta a loose rein. Violetta had calmed down a little but she still danced and spooked as they lapped the outskirts of the arena. Alice gave her a pat. She desperately missed Secret, but she knew this had been her choice. She was riding one of Devon Jenkins' ponies on one of the greatest showgrounds in the country, and she was riding in a team with her friends. She started to feel a buzz of excitement.

"OK?" Devon asked as they walked back up to the stables.

Alice nodded. "I think so," she said. "Thank you so much for this."

"I'm happy to help," Devon smiled, patting her mare. "It's great for her CV and you're going to be brilliant!"

Chapter 14

Alice couldn't stop thinking about the team event as the hours ticked by. She, Mia and her mum had all slept well in the living quarters of the lorry, and were up as the sun rose, ready for Porridge's big moment in the ring. At least the preparation was a good distraction, she thought, as she applied a liberal spray of show conditioner to Porridge's thick black tail. The little Shetland looked amazing, and so did Mia. Mia's mum and dad had just texted to let her know they were on their way to the ring as she swung herself into the saddle.

Alice could tell her own mum was bursting with pride as she fastened her smart jacket up, ready to act as groom in the ring, carrying her wicker basket of grooming products to spruce Porridge up for the in-hand section. Several of Alice's old acquaintances, girls and boys her own age who she'd competed against for years, said hello as they made their way to the arena, many congratulating her on Secret's success. It was strange but nice, Alice thought. She'd never enjoyed showing as much as her mum, but it was rewarding being part of team Porridge and Mia! And later on, as Mia collected a beautiful sixth-place rosette and cantered around in a lap of honour, her hands hurt from clapping so hard. Mia was grinning from ear to ear, delighting the crowd who applauded

loudly, charmed by the little Shetland and his happy rider.

Alice's mum was in a great mood as they all headed back to the stable area, Porridge jogging along, clearly over the moon at being centre of attention.

"Let's hope that bodes well for tomorrow!" she said cheerfully, helping Mia untack and find a bucket and sponge to wipe Porridge down. Slipping away quietly, Alice found Secret, who was whinnying loudly in greeting for his Shetland friend. He nuzzled against Alice as she placed her forehead against his.

"Tomorrow will be different," she said quietly to him. "But I want you to remember everything we've learnt together. And do it for me."

★

The next day, Alice woke long before her alarm. She lay still, listening to the sounds of the show outside the lorry: the early-morning coffee traders, competitors in adjoining lorries getting up and heading to the stables, the smells of breakfast cooking on camping rings drifting over. Peeking out of the cabin window, Alice could see a low-lying mist, the sort that would burn off by nine a.m., revealing yet another beautifully hot summer day.

Her mum, also an early riser, was already up and dressed and nursing a coffee outside.

"Mia!" Alice whispered as she leaned down to the bottom bunk. "Are you up?"

"I don't think I slept," Mia replied back in a nervous voice. "I feel sick."

"Same."

The previous evening's practice had gone OK, but Alice was still finding it hard to get to grips with Violetta. In contrast, Mia and Secret had looked even better than they had the first

time. Jordan and Amy had arrived in a flurry of excitement, along with Angus and June. The team had all enjoyed an impromptu barbecue at Jordan's mum's lorry, and Devon had popped along for a bit, to the delight of the other pony club members. It had been a happy, joyful evening, and Alice had enjoyed every minute. They were a team on and off the arena. She thought briefly back to Chloe and found herself feeling sorry for her.

Dressing quickly, the two girls headed out to the temporary stables where Jordan and Amy were starting to muck out. Amy was a little pale, but Jordan was his usual cheerful self, happily munching on the most enormous bacon sandwich.

Amy groaned, going paler still. "How can you eat that, Jordan?"

"What?" Jordan shrugged. "I'm hungry."

He was definitely the right person to go first, Alice thought. She would be riding third. She and

Angus had had a long chat the previous evening, and had agreed Secret, the most experienced pony on the team would still go last, even with a change of rider. This also gave Mia the longest time to prepare herself. Secret really was the anchor of the team.

It was as if Secret knew things were different today. Devon's groom was mucking out Devon's horses, including Violetta, and so Alice was doing Secret's stable with Mia, and the small act of familiarity was helping her relax. But Secret was restless, walking around his stable, snatching at his hay, and Alice couldn't help the nerves tingling in her fingertips. What if he did play up? But it was too late now. In just a couple of hours she'd be watching her beloved pony take the stage – without her.

★

The warm-up arena was buzzing with excitement

as Hilltops Pony Club made their way forward for the preliminary rounds. Alice knew only the top eight teams would get a chance to jump for a placing in the international arena, and she so hoped they were going to get there! Even if they were eighth, the thrill of being able to jump in the famous ring would be worth it.

As predicted, Jordan jumped a steady first round, going clear to lots of applause. Riding back out, as cool as a cucumber, he high-fived Mia, Amy and Alice in turn.

Angus nodded, not celebrating just yet. "Well done," he said. "Amy, ready?"

And Amy, as white as a sheet, shook her head. Alice knew her friend got nervous before shows, but she'd never seen her look so scared.

"I can't do it!" Amy gasped. "I just can't."

But the team rallied around her.

"You can," Alice said encouragingly. "Just do

your best."

And a moment later Amy nervously rode out into the arena, and everyone collectively held their breath as she started, her lovely pony Whisper clearing fence after fence, until she too had completed the most beautiful clear round. Amy promptly burst into tears. "I did it!"

Then it was Alice's turn. Violetta was wired, each foot dancing in turn, her whole body quivering as Alice nudged her into the arena. Taking a deep breath, she asked Violetta to canter and the mare half reared, bounding forward into the first fence.

Holding on desperately to Devon's words, Alice tried to relax as the warm air whipped tears from her eyes as in a blur of speed Violetta cleared fence after fence. As they came down the final turn to the double, the brown mare cantered in sideways and Alice knew she'd misjudged it, confirmed with a loud rap on the second fence, and she groaned.

One down, when every fault counted.

"And another clear from Hilltops!" the commentator boomed, and Alice glanced behind her. Sure enough, the jump pole remained in place. She breathed a huge sigh of relief. That had been so, so close!

Riding back out, her legs weak with both the adrenalin and the sheer physical exertion of riding such a fiery mare, Alice smiled weakly as Angus congratulated her. She could tell her instructor was trying not to get too excited. Secret and Mia would have to ride clear if they were to stand a chance of getting a place in the finals.

★

"Go on, go on," Alice muttered to herself, crossing her fingers and her toes in her riding boots. If she'd been nervous riding Violetta, it was nothing compared to watching Secret. Secret had looked for her, and there had been no time to get off

Violetta and give him a hug. Alice just had to hope he knew she was there.

Mia was calm, collected and smiling as she nudged Secret into canter. And just as Alice had when she'd watched them jump for the first time, she jumped every single fence alongside them, never taking her eyes off her extraordinary red pony. And as they completed the final double in beautiful style she shut her eyes, breathing out. They'd done it!

"We've got it, everyone." Angus had allowed himself a smile as he quickly totted up scores on his phone. "If I'm right, South Emberside and Langton branches have no time faults. But we're lying in third, so we're going to be in the final." Then, as Mia came back to join them, grinning from ear to ear, he gathered the team around him. "That was the easy bit, the first rounds. But it's going to step up now in the jump-off in the

international arena. *Now* is when you need to ride the best rounds of your life."

★

Time seemed to move both slowly and at lightning speed as the team waited for the finals. There was just long enough to untack and cool their ponies down and grab cold drinks before they needed to walk the jump-off course.

"Whoa," said Mia, clutching Alice's arms as they entered the huge arena. The first round had been challenging, but the jump-off, higher and more technical, was in a different league. It would come down to who out of the eight teams could jump the fastest and best clear rounds. Somehow it seemed twice as vast on foot, and Alice swallowed hard as she gazed up at the imposing stands.

Angus walked with the team, and Alice tried to concentrate on what he was saying. If she'd been riding Secret, she'd know on which parts of the course she'd have to ask for an extra push, where she could safely cut corners. But she didn't know Violetta in the same way. Instead, she talked it through with Mia, and tried as best as she could to explain how she would ride each fence if she was riding Secret. Mia listened intently. Even Jordan had stopped chatting and was chewing his lower lip. Alice's phone beeped and she looked down, and smiled.

Good luck. The message was from Finn. *Wish I was there to cheer you on.*

And so did Alice. She'd never felt so unsure about anything, as if she was teetering on the edge of the unknown, and that unknown was Violetta and the international arena at Hickstead.

★

"OK, team?" Angus smiled round at the team as they gathered at the end of the course walk. "Everyone know what's happening?" He spoke to

everyone, but mostly to Mia, and Alice knew he was making sure she was totally clear about what was to come.

"So all four of you will jump," Angus explained, "but only the best three rounds will count. In order to have the best chance we really need you all to jump clear, or the pressure builds on each rider. OK?"

Alice nodded. With both her and Mia riding ponies they hadn't competed on before, it was a risk. But there was no time to think about it now. They needed to tack up and warm up for the most important jump-off in all of Hilltops' history!

★

Riding back down to the warm-up ring behind the international arena, Alice felt totally surreal. Mia next to her on Secret, and Jordan and Amy on her other side, teammates who'd become good friends – and Violetta's curved ears in front of her, flicking back and forth as she danced from side to side, spooking Secret, who put his ears back and made a face at her.

Gathering around Angus, the team huddled together, nervous smiles passing between them, the air thick with anticipation. As they were lying third, they were third last to jump, the eight teams separated only by fractions of seconds. Alice could barely watch as the first few teams jumped their rounds. The branches were well known, the names familiar from the pages of *Horse & Hound*. It seemed as though the atmosphere had got to a few of the competitors, and those who'd jumped stylish clears in the preliminary rounds were now knocking poles or facing run-outs and refusals. And with each round that passed, the knot in Alice's stomach tightened as she walked Violetta round and round, trying to keep the dark brown mare calm. She couldn't decide if she was more

nervous for herself or Mia!

"OK, guys." Angus clapped his hands. "We're up."

And, as an unusually quiet Jordan rode into the vast arena, time melted away. Angus stood with his hands clenched, never taking his eyes off Jordan who stuck to his usual formula of a steady, safe, clear round, never risking or rushing anything. It wasn't going to be fast, but he'd jumped clear, and Angus nodded, relaxing just a fraction.

"Do your best," he encouraged Amy as Jordan gave Amy the briefest hug as they rode past each other.

To everyone's growing delight Amy, who'd made such huge improvements with her riding that year, jumped her best round ever, and yet again rode out in floods of tears as her mum and dad met her.

"I'm starving," was the first thing she said,

laughing through her tears. "I can't believe I did it!"

And so it was now down to Alice and Mia. So far no other team had managed two clears in a row. If both Alice and Mia managed to jump clear, they were going to be highly placed. But as Alice rode into the arena the jumps seemed to tower above her, and Alice felt a moment of panic. She didn't know this pony at all, she thought wildly. And now she was jumping in one of the most famous arenas in the world! But, taking a deep breath, she barely had to nudge Violetta as the mare sprang forward in a bouncy canter, snatching at her bit, eager to fly over the jumps.

To the outsider looking in Alice was sure they looked fantastic together. But it certainly wasn't the equal partnership she had with Secret. She was just going to have to do her very best. Violetta soared over the first, a deceptively simple-looking

upright that had already had some refusals due to the fact it was on a slight angle and needed careful riding. Galloping on to the next, the big spread and then the first of the doubles disappeared under Violetta's hooves. Halfway round, as Devon had assured Alice, the mare started to relax, but she was strong and Alice's arms were aching with the effort of trying to control her.

Down over the beautiful red-and-white wall and over the oxer, where Violetta cat-leapt, unseating Alice and leaving her precariously unbalanced as she clung on with every bit of strength she had. Secret would have slowed, allowing Alice to right herself, but the action seemed to spook Violetta. Alice rounded the corner down to the last big double, where the sun shone directly in their eyes, and she knew she'd lost control. Violetta took off far too early over the first part, and then slamming on her brakes, skidded into the second part, completely destroying the jumps and sending poles scattering everywhere. Alice almost fell as the crowd gasped and then Violetta lifted her head, allowing Alice to wriggle back into the saddle, feet searching for her stirrups. Thank goodness. A fall would have been instant elimination. As it happened, she had to circle while the stewards hastily rebuilt the second part of the double, allowing Alice to reconnect with Violetta.

"I'm sorry, girl," she whispered, giving the mare an encouraging scratch on the withers. "Let's try again."

This time Alice approached the double steadily, neatly jumping the two fences as the crowd cheered. They'd done it. Alice had ridden a pony she barely knew in the international arena, and although she'd had a fence down and more time faults than she dared to think about, they'd done

their best and it was over. She gave Violetta a hug. The little mare was amazingly talented and would go far with someone who knew her as well as Alice knew Secret.

Angus gave a relieved smile as she rode out. "You made it," he said. "That deserves a prize in itself."

But Alice knew that now the stakes were even higher. The only way they'd get placed was if Mia and Secret jumped a perfect round. She'd so hoped not to be in this position. If she'd jumped clear, the pressure would have eased off Mia. Alice remembered Amy's joking words when Angus had first put together the team. "Secret can pick up the slack!" She'd laughed, but now it really was true. More than ever, everyone was relying on the little red pony.

★

Alice wasn't sure what was worse, watching Mia

209

and Secret, or hiding behind one of the tents, closing her eyes and trying to work out what was happening from the crowd noise. In the end she knew she owed it to Secret to watch. It was as if Secret was searching for her as Mia gathered her reins to ride into the arena. There was just enough time to pause, and Alice leaned right over from Violetta's saddle to hug her pony, before straightening up and nodding at Mia, who nodded back. There was no need for any words. Alice had to let them ride on and know that it was out of her control for the next few minutes.

Secret was popular with the crowd, who burst into applause as he entered, before they were reminded by the commentator to remain silent for the round.

All Alice could do was watch. Without realising it her hands lifted, jumping the first straight bar with Mia, imagining the feel of Secret's plaited

reins, cool between her fingers, the way he felt like
he was about to buck for joy every time after the
first fence. That surge of power down to the next,
feeling the take-off, perfect as always, the spring
between the double, the daring turn just after the
wall, the one no one had attempted yet. But Mia,
who'd been encouraged to do so by Alice during
the course walk, took the chance as a ripple ran
through the crowd and suddenly it looked like
Secret was going to have the fastest time. On over
the next, and the next, and then the final turn down
to the double, where Alice and Violetta had run
into trouble. Alice could tell Secret was startled by
the sunlight.

Come on, boy, come on, come on… She dug her
nails so hard into the palm of her other hand
that she left marks, but she scarcely noticed. Her
breath shortened as Secret jumped the first and,
like a little red Pegasus, flew over the second,

landing to the most tremendous burst of applause. Alice hadn't even realised tears were now pouring down her cheeks. He'd done it. Her brave, loyal red pony had just jumped clear. He'd looked after Mia; he'd done it for Alice. For them all. Alice felt as though her heart was going to burst with love for him.

Chapter 15

Mia seemed dazed as she rode out of the huge arena, looking so young all of a sudden. Everyone gathered around her and she and Secret were swallowed up by a sea of well-wishers, including Mia's mum and dad. Mia's mum was in tears, and so was Alice's mum.

Alice handed Violetta's reins to Jordan and ran over. Secret whickered at the sight of her and, hugging him tightly, Alice pressed her face into his silken mane, breathing in the scent of horse mixed with the lemony tang of fly spray. He'd done it.

"You were brilliant." She smiled up at Mia, wiping her eyes.

Mia shook her head. "No," she said, "I wasn't. Secret was. I just did exactly what you told me; he did the rest. He's amazing – it was the best feeling in the world!"

Hilltops pony club were celebrating quietly even before the last two teams jumped. With the three best scores in place from Jordan, Amy and Mia, they were at least going to be placed third. But as the last eight riders from the final two teams jumped, it soon became apparent they were going to do better than that. Arms round each other's shoulders as they watched, hardly daring to breathe, hoping against hope, as the last rider jumped, her time nowhere near fast enough to

beat Hilltops, Angus turned to the four riders, his face jubilant. "We've done it!"

★

Alice had had some amazing wins in her time, including at Olympia the previous Christmas, but celebrating alongside her three friends felt even better. No one made her feel as though her contribution hadn't counted, even though her final round score had been dropped.

Amy put an arm round her shoulders. "You rode an unknown pony, a tricky one at that, and you did amazingly," she said. "You totally deserve this, with us."

Alice nodded, smiling. She knew Amy was right, but how she longed to be celebrating on Secret! She turned back to Violetta, giving the brown mare a hug, ready to hop back on for the prize-giving.

But then Mia approached, with Secret's reins in her hands.

"He's your pony," she said with a smile, handing over the reins. "You need to ride him in the lap of honour. It wouldn't be right if I rode him. And I'm certainly not riding *her*!" She pulled a face as she gestured at Violetta, who was dancing around. "I'll sit this one out."

After a brief pause, Alice took the reins and Secret nudged her. She could barely speak. "Thank you," she managed at last and Mia laughed.

"Don't be silly!" she said. "I couldn't have done that without you. You've trained the most amazing pony. You ride him now; he's your pony and you deserve it."

Angus, joining them and smiled. "I've cleared it with the officials," he said. "Enjoy it, Alice. It's going to be the first of many rides on him in that arena!"

And so Alice, back in her own saddle, the stirrups let back down, the familiar plaited reins cool in her

hands, the elegant red neck in front of her, finally got to ride in the international arena on her beloved pony. And as she cantered round, savouring every moment as the jewel-green turf disappeared under Secret's powerful canter, enjoying the sight of the crowds between his pricked ears, it really was the best feeling ever. Better than any first place, better than all the ribbons and trophies in the world.

★

Once all the excitement from Hickstead had died down and they were back home, Alice had almost forgotten that Mia was still going to come and help with the general day-to-day jobs at Park Farm. Alice's mum had spent a while planning the summer shows with Mia, and there was talk of her riding some of the other small ponies.

"I loved jumping for the pony club team," Mia had told Alice. "But not as much as I loved being in the show ring!"

Alice felt genuinely delighted. Showing was her mum's first love, and because of Mia's enthusiasm she had a refreshed attitude to it, picking and choosing the best ones to take Mia along to, rather than travelling up and down the country week in and week out.

Glancing at her watch as she filled the last of the hay nets in the late-afternoon sun, Alice threw a handful of hay playfully at Mia . "We'd better go," she smiled. "Race you!"

The girls were heading back to Hilltops for a summer social evening. Mia was now a member of the branch and had made some good friends. As they reached the equestrian centre she waved at a couple of girls before going to join them, soon deep in a huddle of gossip and pony talk.

"Alice!" Amy waved. She looked thoroughly overexcited, and Alice went to join her friend, smiling. She knew that look.

"So, you remember all that stuff with Dupont?" Amy said, as if it had all happened years ago. "You said you'd think about it after Hickstead. Have they been in touch? What do you think? Are you up for more shoots and publicity and stuff?"

Alice took a deep breath. Dupont had featured the photo in the latest edition of *Horse & Hound*. But Alice had made up her mind. One shoot had been just about fine, but that had been enough for her!

She shook her head. "I'm not going to do any more."

Amy groaned loudly. "But you'd do so well, Al! Think of all the publicity!"

But Alice had to remain true to herself. "It's not for me," she said firmly, taking a deep breath. "Actually, Amy," she continued, "do you mind if we step back from all the online Secret stuff?

You've been amazing with it, but I think I've had enough."

Amy stopped in her tracks. "Do I have to stop doing it completely?" she said, looking horrified.

Alice shook her head. "No," she said. "But let's just take it a bit easy? Perhaps update it occasionally…" She hesitated. "All this stuff with Chloe made me realise I don't like people thinking they know me, when they're only getting a tiny glimpse of me and my life. It doesn't feel right."

"OK," Amy agreed. "If that's what you want."

Alice nodded and gave her friend a hug. "It is. Thanks, Amy."

Hilltops' victory was still the talk of the pony club. The huge cup they'd won was in the café, alongside a lovely photo of the four riders and their ponies. Alice and Mia both had their arms round Secret! Angus and June had had several new membership enquiries and *Horse & Hound* were

going to feature the branch in their next edition.

"Oooh!" Amy nudged Alice as they made their way over to the barbecue. "There's Devon! What's she doing here?"

Looking up, Alice blinked. Amy was totally right. There was Devon, casually dressed in shorts and a white shirt, talking to Angus and June.

Spotting Alice, she smiled and waved. "Hi! Just the person I wanted to see."

"Go on," Amy smiled, giving Alice a gentle push forward.

"Alice," June said warmly, "Devon has some exciting news."

★

"So let me get this straight," Finn repeated, and Alice smiled, pressing the phone closer to her ear.

She'd taken Secret up to the top of the downs and had stopped at the highest point, the hills bathed in a pink glow as the sun started to creep upwards in the sky as the dawn broke. It was her favourite time to ride. But this morning she'd broken the silence and rung Finn. The news was too amazing not to share!

"Devon wants you to go there, to her yard, with Secret, for training?" Finn continued. "And you're actually going for try-outs?"

"For the pony internationals," Alice said, rolling the words luxuriously around. It still felt surreal, as it had done since the previous evening when Devon had come to Hilltops. "I'm trying out for the GB team! Devon has something to do with the young rider squad; she doesn't select but she trains, and she wanted to tell me in person when she heard about it."

"Wow," Finn said, sounding so far away but right next to Alice at the same time. "That's amazing, Alice. You have to go for it!"

"Not even a question," Alice said determinedly.

She believed in Secret more than ever now. Seeing him jump with Mia had only cemented that – she was so proud of him and of herself. And now they had their whole future ahead of them. Whether it was the international arena at Hickstead, the fields of home or the unknown challenge ahead of the GB pony try-outs, she'd always see the future between those red ears. And there was no place else on Earth she'd rather be.

Acknowledgements

Thank you to the wonderful team at Nosy Crow, in particular Kirsty and Fiona for all their expert help and guidance and Nic and Ray for their amazing design skills and for producing the most beautiful covers. A huge thank you to my lovely editor Sarah who totally 'got' Finn and Alice from the start and has been amazing to work with. And thanks to the whole team at Nosy Crow who support the books so brilliantly from start to finish!

Special thanks to Jolie Darton, former owner of Butler – our beautiful cover star. Jolie made sure Butler looked like a superstar ready for his photo shoot! Good luck in your new home, Butler!

Finally, writing pony books really is the best job in the world and I must thank my husband Clive who supports me every step of the way despite his own very busy job running the family farm. And of course my children Lara, whose love for ponies mirrors my own, and sweet Jasper who smiles all day.

If you enjoyed this book, look out
for the rest of the series!

Here's a peek at the first book…

A New
Beginning

OLIVIA TUFFIN

PROLOGUE

The Highland gelding was snow white in colour, and his thick mane fell perfectly, each and every tangle carefully combed out. "That's better," the boy smiled, giving the pony a pat. When he was with his horse the boy could forget everything, all of the heartbreak from the last year, all of the worry that lay ahead. Lost in thought, he gave a start as someone came into the stable next to him.

The man was on the phone and clearly unaware his every word could be heard. Keeping as still as possible, his pony's ears pricked up and the boy felt his blood run cold.

"She's got to be loaded. She inherited this place!" The man was laughing. "And yet she's putting everything into this stupid team. 'Oh, here come the Flying Fillies!'" he mocked. "But the ponies are top quality, and could be worth a lot in the right hands…"

There was a pause, then another peal of harsh laughter.

"Working on it." The man's voice was gleeful. "As soon as I persuade her to ditch this dump of a yard and her weird brother. Give me time…"

The stable door banged and the voice faded away. The boy could breathe again.

Placing a trembling hand on his pony's mane, the boy held his head up high. He would do all he

could to protect everything he loved so dearly: the ponies, this yard, his home and his beloved Flying Fillies.

They had an event that afternoon, and as always they would plaster on their smiles. If only those watching knew exactly what it was like when the music stopped.

★
★
★

Chapter 1

Thirteen year old Alice Smalley patted the neck of her red roan pony, Secret, as he stood quietly during a championship class. It had been another successful day for her mum's show team. Alice loved every one of the horses at Park Farm, the family's competition yard, but it was Secret who held a special place in her heart.

She smiled as Secret flicked an ear back, as

if listening to her thoughts. The bond between the two was unbreakable. Secret had been hard work – he was stubborn and headstrong – but Alice had worked tirelessly training him, and her effort was paying off. Now, at almost six years of age, the future was looking very bright for the talented gelding.

The judge smiled, calling the pair forward into first place. No one was surprised; Secret was a born show pony. He'd inherited the good looks of his dam, Lily, and the flamboyant personality of his sire, Carlamu Rowan. Secret didn't just trot, he *floated*. When he entered the ring his eyes sparkled and he lapped up the attention. The bigger the audience, the better he performed.

"Redgrove Secret," the commentator said over the loudspeaker, "trained and produced by Alice Smalley!"

Grinning, Alice nudged her pony into a

canter, Secret's long strides eating up the ground and his crimson mane flying. The crowd clapped and cheered, full of admiration for the real-life red Pegasus and his talented rider...

"*Alice!*" Josephine Smalley's shrill voice cut sharply through Alice's thoughts, and she jumped, feeling guilty. "All OK?" Josephine peered at her daughter, and then, without waiting for an answer, was back to business. "Come on," she said bossily, "there's still Lachlan's second class to go and you need to hurry. Go, and good luck!"

Alice sighed heavily. She had been completely lost in her daydream. But here she was at the side of the ring, clutching the reins of Porridge, her faithful Shetland. Secret was still out in his paddock at home. He was nowhere near ready for a championship class, and Alice knew it. There were days she couldn't even get him to walk *into* an arena, even in hand, let alone canter

around one as the winner, and so far every show they had attended to had been a disaster one way or another.

Automatically Alice's hand touched the curved pink scar on her cheek, as it did whenever she thought about how the little gelding had come to her. If it hadn't been for Secret, Alice would never have gone near a horse again. The scar would always remind her of her accident with Honey, the worst day of her life. A simple cross-country ride on a crisp Christmas Eve had ended in tragedy after Honey had fallen at a jump and died, and Alice had been badly injured. It had been no one's fault; Honey's big heart had simply given up. Over time the memory had grown easier to live with, but Alice owed Secret everything.

Alice gave Porridge a final pat before sprinting off to complete her last ridden class, trying not to roll her eyes. Show days were everything to her mum, and she was always uptight.

Josephine Smalley, Alice's mum, was a highly respected showing producer, and Alice had played a big part in the yard's success, winning just about every championship out there. There was a long waiting list of people who were desperate to send her mum their best ponies to train and compete. As a result, Alice always had wonderful ponies to ride. A few riders on the circuit resented this, saying that Alice only had to sit there and collect rosettes, and that it didn't take any real skill. So Alice was desperate to prove herself both as a good rider *and* as a trainer, and Secret was her chance. The little roan was hers, and hers alone. But Alice had to admit she was struggling with the spirited red pony.

Moments later, mounted on Lachlan, a magnificent Highland, Alice's thoughts drifted to her mum. Alice often wished she could have a

regular pony club mum, and that they had time for other stuff, like fun rides and cross-country rallies. But ever since Alice's fall Josephine had been cautious about Alice doing anything risky. Alice often thought back to how alive and free she had felt galloping cross-country on her beloved mare, right before her world had come crashing down. She had very nearly given up riding for good, and it had only been the chance arrival of Secret that had encouraged her back to her true love, ponies.

A few years had passed since then, and Alice had qualified numerous ponies for the Horse of the Year Show and Olympia. Every spare surface in the Smalley's kitchen was covered with sashes and rosettes. Josephine lived and breathed showing, taking ponies all over the country to compete in flat ridden classes. Her speciality was mountain and moorland classes, where the ponies competed against others of the same breed.

★
★
★

It required a huge amount of work to school the ponies to this high standard, and most weekends were spent riding them at the shows.

But Alice was growing tired of the show ring. It wasn't that she didn't enjoy riding the ponies, but showing was never what Alice had been into. Before her fall she had been hoping to join the local pony club. But Alice's confidence had taken such a knock that it had seemed simpler to help her mum out and concentrate solely on the showing. Now that's all she did: the same thing week after week.